VALENTINE VOWS

BOOK THREE OF THE MISSED CONNECTIONS
TRILOGY

KATHRYN REIGN

CONTENTS

VALENTINE VOWS

BOOK THREE OF THE MISSED CONNECTIONS TRILOGY

KATHRYN REIGN

1

DAMASCUS

I really care for Blair, this incredible girl I'm seeing. I want to do whatever I can to make sure I get to keep seeing her. And Blair said that Jennifer, my ex-girlfriend who I used to be heartbroken over—but I'm feeling much better about the whole thing these days, now that I have Blair—can't be a part of my life if we're going to make our relationship work, and I completely agree with that.

So, when Jennifer finds me strolling around the

waterfront with a coffee in my hand, I'm fully prepared to tell her to get lost. And for the first time ever, I feel nothing toward her when I see her approaching. There are no butterflies. No pain from the hurt she caused in my chest.

There's absolutely nothing.

"Are you following me?" I ask her as I lean against the railing over the water and glare at her.

Blair's college winter break is going to be over soon, and she has some assignments that she has to get done, so she's working hard in the library and told me she'll meet up with me after. We've been Snapchatting with each other back and forth. She sent me a photo of herself pouting in her study cubicle and saying she wished she was with me, so I sent her a photo of me holding my coffee in front of the boats, telling her I missed her. Then three seconds later, the she-devil appears.

"I was having brunch with Hannah," Jennifer explains in her velvety voice, her long dark hair tossed behind her shoulders as she points to the restaurant down the way. Hannah is one of her best friends. "I saw you through the window." She reaches me completely and stops walking.

"Cool. I don't want to talk to you."

"Damascus, come on." She crosses her arms. It's probably infuriating to her that I won't do whatever she wants like I used to. She's not the one I want to make happy anymore. It's all about my beautiful, red-headed Blair.

"No, *you* come on. I'm serious. You're a horrible

human being."

"*I* am?"

"Dude. You dumped me because I go to therapy. I'm sorry, but that's pretty messed up."

"What do you mean, *therapy*?" she asks. "That girl you were with when I ran into you the other day, my dad had you followed because he didn't trust you. He got multiple photos of you and her together. I didn't even know you were *in* therapy."

I step away from the railing. "Wait. You dumped me because you thought I was cheating on you with *Leah*?"

"You guys were hugging and laughing in a bunch of the photos! And you never told me you were hanging out with her!"

"Why did you tell me you dumped me because you were just using me to get at your dad, then?" I had been absolutely crushed when I thought she had never really felt anything for me at all. Now she's trying to tell me that she had feelings for me all along?

"Because! I didn't want you to know that I was hurt. And… I figured you would think it was me who had you followed and not my dad if I told you how I found out."

"So, you lied?"

"Who is she, then?" Jennifer asks, not answering my question. "Why didn't you ever tell me about her? Are you trying to tell me that you were never with her?"

I can't believe this.

"No, I was never with her! If you had thought to take one simple second to ask me about it, you would have found that out! She is my support group leader!"

All this time, both of our hearts were broken over

each other because of a simple miscalculation. Jennifer hadn't been using me. All this time, Jennifer has been missing me, too. All this time, she had loved me after all.

"I messed up, Dam."

I nod, not knowing how to respond. I would have never lost her if we had been better at communicating. Months we've spent without each other, hurting when we didn't have to be.

Jennifer steps closer to me. "I am so sorry. I didn't know. I love you, Damascus. I never stopped for a second."

I'm trying to think of what to say back when she leans in and kisses me. I am so surprised by the familiarity of her lips. The nostalgia of hearing her tell me that she loves me. I am overwhelmed by the fact that our relationship hadn't been a sham. All of it makes it impossible for me to *not* kiss her back.

When we pull away, I look behind her and see my girlfriend. She's standing on the other side of the street with her backpack, her face twisted in pain.

"Shit," I breathe. Jennifer turns to look, too. Blair quickly runs in the other direction, away from us.

I don't call to her. I don't tell Jennifer off and chase after her. I don't do anything about it at all.

I *wanted* to do whatever it took to make sure that Blair and I stayed together.

But I guess I'm just incapable.

2

GISELLE

"Don't you like it?" Steve asks. He's my fake boyfriend, blackmailing me into dating him unless I want him revealing photos to the world of married fashion designer, Eliza Leon, and me, an A-list supermodel, kissing.

I push my salmon around on my plate at the restaurant we're at. It's some fancy place in West Hollywood on a rooftop, with a plant-lined patio and incredible city views.

I shrug at Steve and say nothing.

He sighs heavily, runs his hand through his short blonde hair, and puts his fork down. He had told me that his Wagyu steak is one of the best things he's ever tasted, so I don't know why he suddenly lost his appetite for it.

"What's wrong?" I ask.

"Nothing." But it's clearly *something*.

The entire rest of our lunch, Steve keeps his head down and doesn't say a word to me. Usually, we're speaking to each other through fake smiles and tossing insults around about how he's crazy and how I like girls. Sometimes I forget that he blackmailed me, and we end up actually having fun together. Besides, being with Steve prevents people from wondering if I wished I were with a woman, instead. So, if I really think about it, we need each other.

When we pay our tab and head to the elevator, Steve doesn't even try to hold my hand.

"Okay, what's going on with you?" I ask again. We are alone, so he's allowed to be real with me right now.

"I'm fine, Giselle."

"No, you aren't," I say. "You didn't talk to me at all during lunch. And now you're not even trying to get me to hold your hand. Something is up."

When he looks at me now, his expression is hurt. "What? Have you started to actually wish I *would* hold your hand?"

I hold my hand against my chest and frown. "Well, no, but…"

The elevator door opens, and we step out. Immediately, a small crowd approaches to ask for my autograph. Even as I smile at them and make light conversation, Steve just stands there with a blank look on his face. Usually when fans are around, he acts extra lovey-dovey with me, wanting to show the world how "happy" we both are.

When we're in my precious lavender Porsche, he opens the door for me, and then slams it shut when I get in. Then he climbs in on the passenger side.

"I don't think I can drive anywhere until you tell me what's going on," I tell him.

"I think you're amazing, Giselle," he says. He faces forward and refuses to look at me. He always keeps up with having his hair bright and blonde, but looking closer at it, I am noticing that he hasn't touched up his roots recently. This is also unlike him.

"Okay…" I trail off.

"I hoped our agreement would have helped you think that I was amazing, too."

"I thought you were amazing before you decided to blackmail me," I point out. "You were one of my favorite people to hang out with." It's true. I met him during a modeling gig that he was working, and we instantly became friends.

Now, we're… this.

"I also thought if we dated, maybe I would learn more about the real you and realize that you're not anything close to the mental image I had made up of you in my head." Still, he doesn't meet my eyes. "But that didn't work. You're better than I pictured. Smart. Funny. Charming. Giving. The way you spoiled your family on Christmas and acted equally excited about the lame stuff they got you. I… it only made me fall in love with you."

"In *love* with me?" I ask, my hands on the steering wheel even though we aren't going anywhere. "I don't understand."

Steve sniffs, and that's when I realize why he won't look at me. He's crying. "I don't either. I just wanted so badly for you to feel something for me. Anything."

"Steve, that day that you caught Eliza and me in the stairwell. You saw the whole thing, right?"

"I didn't hear everything she said to you, or what you said to her. I just heard the last bit of it and watched her kiss you."

And you took a photo of it, I want to add. "So, you saw that *she* kissed *me*, right?"

He nods.

"I don't know what you think about it, like maybe you thought I was just confused. Or maybe you thought Eliza had feelings for me but that I didn't return them." I can feel myself starting to sweat, and for a moment, I'm confused as to why. But then I think about it. In a way, Steve is the first person I've ever come out to. I continue. "But I have known for a long time that I am not straight."

Finally, Steve looks at me. "You mean, like, there isn't a single ounce of you that is attracted to men?"

I shake my head and feel liberated. "No. I don't know why, and I don't know how. That's just the way my brain works. It has nothing to do with who I think you are as a person."

"So, if you weren't gay…?"

"If I wasn't… *gay*, I probably *would* have agreed to go on a date with you. You make me laugh. You are amazing at giving me compliments, and you know how much I love them. You make me feel like I'm doing the right thing by modeling. You make me feel like I'm good enough. *And* you're super freaking talented."

He smiles the tiniest bit. "So, you would be interested in the girl version of me?"

"Why, do you have a sister?" We look at each other for a moment, then both of us giggle before I continue. "Of course, I thought all these things about you *before* you forced me to date you. I'm not sure what I think about you anymore." I might as well continue being honest.

Steve runs both of his hands over his face. "I don't know what I was thinking, Giselle. I was just doing things without taking a second to stop and process them. I hate who I have become."

I put a hand on his shoulder. "Then change it," I tell him. "We're in LA. People literally change their personalities every single day. You can be whoever you want to be."

"I suppose you're right." He pats the hand I have on his shoulder. "Giselle, I think it's time we break up."

I beam at him, proud of how he decided to behave about this. Maybe I don't have to completely hate him after all.

"I think that might be a good idea."

3

KENNETH

I never want to come down from this high.

First, Leah Olson, the quiet ex-girlfriend of the quasi-famous college football player, Derek Heed, tells me that she's going to give me an exclusive on Heed's abuse. Domestic abuse. Then the game that everyone predicted Derek's team winning turned out to go the exact opposite way, and now their season is over.

Honestly, I wonder if I should play the lottery.

After Leah and I met officially for the first time

yesterday, we decided that, today, she would come to the house I'm temporarily living in so that we have privacy while I do my interview with her, as the celebrity journalist that I am.

Then after she walked away, I called my jerk of a boss, Rainer Wilkinson, to give him the good news. He seemed doubtful of whether or not I was telling the truth, which I guess I don't blame him for. But either way, my job is going to be saved because of this wonderful random woman. Because without a juicy story on Derek Heed, Rainer basically told me I didn't need to bother going back to LA.

When Leah comes over, I whip the door open with a wide smile. Leah is in her mid-twenties, has fair skin, dark brown hair to her waist, and haunting blue eyes. Eyes that say they've had a hard life, even when her mouth speaks nothing.

I can tell that Leah is trying to hide smile in return. "Someone is awfully happy," she points out.

I step aside. "Come in, come in. Sorry, but I've been waiting for a day like this."

"I often have wondered if it's every man's dream to have a girl tell him all about how she was abused in high school." Leah's tone is light and joking, but it makes me feel bad, nonetheless. She comes inside, and I shut the door behind her.

"I'm so sorry that I am being an idiot. It's messed up, what he did to you."

Leah makes herself comfortable on the couch. "I know. That's why we're going to make him pay." Rumors have been circulating about how Derek Heed is a girlfriend abuser, ever since Selena and I decided to anonymously make a post about it that went viral on social media. I could have easily gotten a story from Selena, Derek's wife, to give to my antsy, impatient boss, but Selena didn't want anyone knowing that she was the one who revealed the truth about Derek. And I don't want to double-cross her. I wouldn't dream of it.

I grab a dining chair and drag it into the living room so I can sit across from her with my notepad and recorder. "Exactly." Leah's story couldn't come at a more perfect time. The hype about Derek being a potential wife-beater is dying down in the media. This story is going to be the perfect way to get negative attention brought back to him.

"So… Are you ready to do this?" I ask.

She holds her finger up. "Hold on one sec." She takes her phone out of her back pocket and goes to type up something to someone. "Sorry, I just promised I would tell Selena when I was here."

My mouth goes dry, and my stomach flips at the mere mention of Selena's name. "You… you know Selena?"

"Well, yeah. Who do you think told me that I should talk to you if I want to do an interview?"

I smile. "I definitely owe her one, then." My cheeks are starting to hurt from how big I'm smiling. Leah notices it and gives me a strange look. I try to compose myself and put my serious interview face on.

"You really like her, don't you?" Leah guesses.

I'm quick to wave it off. "She is a good person. I care about her."

"How often do you get to see her?"

"For a while, it was every day," I admit. "But she's visiting her parents across the country right now."

Leah nods and looks like she wants to ask more, but I have to stop her. "Wait a second, aren't *I* supposed to be the one giving the interview?"

She snaps her jaw shut and nods. I start the questions.

4

DAMASCUS

So, I got back together with Jennifer. I hadn't expected this ever happening, but here we are. I hate that I hurt Blair, but the only reason Jennifer and I ever stopped dating in the first place was because of a misunderstanding. Now that it's all cleared up, we can be together again. I had spent six months dreaming for this, so I owed it to myself to accept her when she finally came back to me.

"Happy Valentine's Day!" Jennifer shouts at me the

second she walks into my apartment. In her arms, she has a massive fuzzy brown teddy bear. It's nearly the size of her.

I roll my eyes. "Jennifer, what the hell is that?" She hands me the bear, and I set it on the floor.

Jennifer pouts. "It's your Valentine's Day present!"

I go to retort.

She beats me to it. "I know, I know. We said no presents. I just figured you meant no *expensive* presents."

"I told you I hate this holiday. I meant no presents of any cost."

She rolls her eyes at me and kisses me on the lips. Over in the kitchen, Sara and Andy are making breakfast together, and I don't miss it when they give each other a grossed-out look. They no longer like Jennifer. Not after having to deal with what she did to me. I don't blame them. But I've had to tell Jennifer multiple times that they'll come around.

"So, I'm guessing that means you didn't actually get me anything," Jennifer says. I shrug and shake my head. "It's just a regular day for me," I try.

"So, no dinner reservations anywhere? No candles or romance?"

I wrinkle my nose at her. "I don't think I've ever made a reservation at any restaurant."

She hangs on me and looks into my eyes. "Fine, we'll stay in tonight. Will you at least go get us some alcohol and cigarettes?"

I've never smoked, and I rarely ever drank when I was with Blair, but it's crazy how quickly I fell back into my old habits as soon as Jennifer and I started dating again. Now it's back to being rebellious, and drinking and partying almost every night of the week.

"Fine. But it's just going to be a normal night, right?"

I had already discussed this with Blair when we were dating. I told her that it would be more meaningful if I got her flowers and random gifts on random days to show her how I felt about her. She thought it made complete sense and said she had always hated the holiday. She thought it was mean that other couples flashed their love while some people were lonely.

I hope she's not lonely today.

Jennifer lets go of me and waves her hand. "Yeah, yeah, yeah. Whatever Mr. Grumpy Pants wants."

Andy and I exchange a look. I can tell what he's thinking: that I should be with Blair and not her. But I was never going to get Blair back. There was no point in even trying. I hurt her too much. The second she ran away from me the day she saw me kissing Jennifer, she blocked me on all forms of contact.

Honestly, it's for the best. I'm not good enough for her. I was an idiot for thinking I ever could be.

5

———

BRENNAN

If there's any day of the year to make a big gesture, wouldn't Valentine's Day be considered one of the best ones?

I don't exactly know how I feel about Leah Olson, and I don't know how she feels about me. All I know is that I can't stop thinking about her. I just want to clear the air with her so that she can feel better about what happened on Christmas Eve between us. I can't stand the thought of her being afraid of me.

Leah is the ex of my older brother, Derek. And according to her, Derek abused her in high school. Badly. So much so that Leah practically swore of men forever, and now she runs multiple group therapy classes. On somewhat of a random whim, I ended up hanging out with Leah and her family, doing a bar crawl all of Christmas Eve. Then when it was over, Leah was incredibly drunk, and me, being the mainly sober one, was asked by Leah to take care of her and stay at her apartment.

But then, when Leah woke up in the morning, she didn't remember any of it and had screamed at me to get the hell out. I later came to find out, from my brother's wife, Selena, that Leah had been terrified that I might have taken advantage of her while she was in her drunken state. Something that definitely had *not* happened.

It doesn't take me too much digging to go to the town center's website and figure out what days Leah's support groups are being held. Then this morning, I went to the grocery store and grabbed her a bouquet of flowers—bright, spring-looking ones—because I figured red roses were too romantic. Now that that's done, I'm in the car, driving to the building where she works. From there, I get out and stand outside in the freezing cold until her sessions are over for the day.

She's alone when she comes out, carrying a binder and a notebook with her purse over her shoulder. She's looking down at her phone while she walks, and when she looks up and sees me standing there, she freezes.

I'm nervous, but I don't care. I want to do this.

"What is this?" Leah asks me, looking behind her like maybe I'm waiting for somebody else instead.

"I am so sorry about Christmas," I say. I can't believe it's already been almost two full months since the last time I had spoken to her. And I can't believe I've thought about her every single day since.

"Brennan," she sighs in warning.

"Leah, I just want to apologize. And I'd like to get the chance to explain myself to you. But if you don't want me to, you can tell me, and I will stop talking right now and walk away." I don't want to push this on her. I am *not* Derek.

She hesitates. "Did you really buy me flowers?"

"They're apology flowers," I reassure her.

We're still a safe distance away from each other, so I don't reach out and try to give them to her. I'm still waiting for her answer.

"It's really okay, Brennan. You didn't have to do this."

"But I want to. I've been upset about it for weeks."

"Why?"

"Because I had an amazing time with you and your family on Christmas Eve. I like being around you. And I never realized that having a guy in your house was such a big deal. I would have never disrespected you like that otherwise."

"Of course, you didn't know. How could you have?"

I step toward her. "Still. I just really need you to know that nothing happened. You threw up in the toilet, and so I made sure you were okay. You asked me to stay, so I did. But I was almost sober. I knew better than to think that maybe I was going to get lucky or something. The only reason my shirt was off is because I used it as a pillow since you were hogging all of them."

This gets a hint of a smile on her face, and it warms my heart. She steps closer to me. "I… I think I knew deep down that nothing happened. I overreacted, and it was embarrassing. So, I figured it was probably for the best, anyway. I figured you probably thought I was crazy, and that the only reason we ever started talking was because of your brother, so I guess I didn't really see the point in reaching back out. You had gotten all of the information I could give you. I didn't think there was any more reason for us to keep talking to each other."

I raise my eyebrows. "Ouch."

"I'm sorry. Christmas Eve was a lot of fun. I think the only reason I ended up getting so drunk was because I wanted you to like me. I wanted to be fun and loose and seem like I was down for anything."

"You can be yourself around me. I like you regardless."

"Brennan, I think you and I both know there is something between us. I have thought about you every single day since Christmas, too."

I take another step toward her, an encouraging smile on my face. But she shakes her head.

"I just—sorry, I don't know why this is so hard—I-I have feelings for you. But it scares the hell out of me. I know it's messed up, but it's true. I can't stop thinking that you might turn out like your brother." Tears well in her eyes as I stand there with my mouth hanging open in disbelief.

"Leah. I…"

"Sometimes it's hard to even look at you. Because I see him. And it sucks."

It's funny because my entire life, I had always considered it a compliment to be compared to Derek. Now I feel like I've never been madder about it. Leah and I will never be anything because she will never be able to look past my brother. It makes sense. I don't know why I even bothered.

"I am sor—" she starts.

I drop the flowers by my side. "Don't worry about it," I say, turning to leave. "Good job on the interview with Kenneth. I bought the magazine as soon as I heard. It's too bad Selena still went back to Derek."

I'm surprised that she calls out my name when I walk away, but I don't turn back to her. At the nearest trashcan, I drop the flowers inside. Then I stick my hands in my jacket pockets and keep my head down as I go.

6

GISELLE

I'm going to spend Valentine's Day with my friends. We're going to have an anti-boy night —ha-ha on my part—and watch rom-coms and eat healthy snacks disguised as junk food. I am not going to see Eliza, despite how badly I wish I could. I will let her enjoy this day with Shawn.

But then imagine my surprise, when around three o'clock—as I'm at the grocery store getting the supplies for girls' night—Eliza calls me.

"Happy love day!" I say when I answer, trying to sound upbeat.

"Shawn is in the hospital."

I gasp. "Is he okay?"

"I don't know. I'm here now, waiting. It was awful. I just… I would love to see you. Is there any chance you would want to come meet me?"

"See you? Yeah. I… I'll head to the hospital now. Text me the address."

I guess there's been a change of plans.

I MEET Eliza outside of Shawn's hospital room. Bryan lingers down in the distance, making himself comfortable on a bench. Eliza's eyes are bloodshot, and she keeps pacing back and forth.

The moment she sees me, she races over and throws her arms around me. I hug her tightly, worried about Shawn. "Any news?"

"They think it might be time for the chair," she informs me. She's referring to the chair like Stephen Hawking had. Eliza and Shawn were investing in the best one that money could buy. It would give him the ability to communicate through a computer when he is no longer able to speak.

"I'm so sorry," I say. What else can you say in a situation like this? What else is there? No one wants to be told that it will be fine. No one wants to be told, *look on the bright side*. What's happening to Shawn is devastating.

Eliza says nothing. She just keeps hugging me.

AFTER STAYING at the hospital with Eliza until almost nine at night, I feel like I need to do something to cheer her up. Valentine's Day isn't over yet. Shawn is going to be in the hotel hospital overnight so they can run more tests and get him situated, and one of the doctors even told Eliza that it would be a good idea for her to get outside for a little while.

"Where are we going?" Eliza asks as I drive her new Lamborghini through the city.

"You'll see." I go to her favorite Thai restaurant and run inside with my sunglasses on to pick up our order. Already, when I get back in the car, she's ten times happier than she had been at the hospital. It makes my stomach dip at the sight of her smile.

"Sorry for the pit-stop," I say. Then I resume driving her car back to my apartment. I pull into the garage and park in my guest spot, then I grab the food, and the two of us walk to the penthouse.

I really hope I gave Iris enough time, I think to myself. I am slow to put my key in the knob, just in case. Then when I open it, Eliza is greeted by candles lit up every-where. A lot of them are fake because of the fire hazard, of course, but it looks incredible in here regardless. Next to me, Eliza has a hand to her heart.

"How did you do this?" she asks.

So, maybe a little part of me had wondered if she would ask to come over and want to spend Valentine's Day with me instead of Shawn after all. Sue me. I just had my assistant on standby to set this up in case it happened. She is single anyway, and I told her I would pay her overtime.

I try to be mysterious as I smile at Eliza. "I have my ways." I take her hand and bring her over to my living area. There are rose petals everywhere—real ones—along with chocolates and candy hearts, and lots of red and pink soft fuzzy blankets and pillows. Her favorite romance movie is already queued up on the TV screen —*Titanic*. A bottle of her favorite wine is freshly poured into two glasses.

I set the Thai food bag on the coffee table and take Eliza's hands in mine. "I hope it's not too much," I say. "I had every intention of leaving you alone today."

She leans in and kisses me on the lips, making me so happy that I step closer and wrap my arms around her. I think about Eliza's lips every other second, every single day.

She smiles at me when we pull apart. "I had those intentions as well. But it seems that no matter what I do, Giselle, I will never be able to stay away from you."

7

———

KENNETH

The way somebody pounds on my door at my rental makes my heart stop. I immediately assume that it's Derek, here to beat the hell out of me for keeping Selena hidden in my house for so long.

I don't move from my spot on the couch. Maybe if I don't answer it, he will just go away.

"Kenneth!"

Wait a second. That's a woman's voice.

I leap up from the couch and race over to the door. I

swing it open, expecting to see Selena, and my heart falls when I see Leah instead. She looks windswept and out of breath. Pounding on my door has really done a number on her.

"Leah?" I ask in confusion.

"I'm sorry to barge in on you like this," she says, brushing aside me to enter my house. "But I need to tell you something."

I close the door and turn to her. "What's going on?" My heart is pounding because I think she's about to tell me that Derek retaliated against her for my interview. I can't have that on my conscience. I don't know what I will do if something happens to Leah because of me.

"You told me Selena went back to her parents," Leah says.

"Yeah?"

"I know how she was staying here. She told me about it. I didn't tell you because I didn't know if you would be mad that she hadn't kept it a secret. But the thing is… She *didn't* go back to her parents. I don't really know what's going on because she won't talk to me, but Kenneth… She went back to Derek."

My mouth keeps opening and closing. "She… Her parents… *Derek?*"

She sits down on my couch and brings her feet up. "Yes. I don't know what's happening. Or why she lied to you."

"How do you know this?" I walk over and sit down on the coffee table.

"Brennan. He told me himself."

I don't understand it. Why did Selena go back? Did

she miss him? Did she think he would change? I know Derek had been making a lot of Instagram accounts in order to try and contact her. I wonder if maybe Selena finally caved?

"I just don't get it," I say to Leah. "I never saw her at the stadium. Or around town. Does she just never leave the house?"

"I don't know. I guess you never really know what the inside of a relationship is like."

"Do you think she loves him?" I ask without thinking. Jesus, why do I even care? She went back to him. No matter what Derek does to her, she's not going to leave him. I don't know why I didn't see it before.

Leah sighs. "She might be confused. Derek is incredible at manipulation. It's hard to tell."

I could have told her how I felt on New Year's Eve. I could've had a completely different conversation with her than I did.

My phone buzzes on the coffee table with a text. I pick it up, hoping it's Selena telling me to rescue her. But of course, it's not. It's my boss, Rainer, telling me more positive feedback on my article in Sunwest Weekly. Thanks to me, Derek is trending all over again, and not in a good way.

Leah quickly hops to her feet. "Anyway, I should go. Sorry again for coming here unannounced. I know it's Valentine's Day and all that."

"No, I'm glad you came by. Thank you for letting me know." I get up with her and walk her to the door. "Hey, Derek hasn't tried to reach out to you since the article posted, has he?"

She smiles at me. "Not once. I'm really glad I did it, you know that?"

I return the smile. I'm glad she did, too. "Well, enjoy your Valentine's Day. Spend it with someone you love."

"Yeah, and you have fun… doing whatever it was you were doing before I came here." We laugh a little, and I close the door. Back over on my coffee table, my phone is ringing. I run over, again hoping it's Selena.

It's Steve. Sighing, I answer it. "What's up, stud? You calling me to tell me you love me?" I joke.

"Happy Valentine's Day, baby," he says. "I'm *dying* over here, Kenny."

"What's going on? You and Giselle Cosgrove okay?"

"We broke up. "It wasn't even real."

I try to be sympathetic. "Oh, come on, you had a good run."

"No. The whole relationship wasn't real. I did something horrible in order to get her to date me."

"Wait, what do you mean?"

"What I am about to tell you is a lot. And it's off the record, okay? I mean it. No one can ever know."

Great, more juicy stuff I can't impress my boss with. "Just tell me."

"I caught Giselle kissing Eliza Leon. I took a photo of it and used it against her."

I hadn't, in *any* way, been anticipating that this story would have any implication on my life. But Giselle and my stepmom?

What the fuck is going on?

8

DAMASCUS

I didn't mean to get drunk and accidentally stroll down my ex-girlfriend's street. I had been walking aimlessly with no goal in mind. I swear. Now that I'm back with Jennifer, I don't even need to think about Blair anymore. Hopefully, she's met somebody else. A good boy in one of her classes who will give her everything she wants in life.

I don't plan on stopping when I get to Blair's house.

I just want to see if her car is there. See if she is home. Imagine her sitting by a warm fire, working on all of her assignments. Maybe the supermodel, Giselle Cosgrove, is in town visiting.

I focused on staring up into the bedroom windows of the second floor, wondering if Blair could sense my appearance. Maybe any second now, there'd be a crack in her blinds, and she would notice me.

"Are you Damascus?"

I snap my head around to whoever just spoke to me. Then a woman about Blair's height, maybe even shorter, stands up from the rosebush that she had been trimming. I hadn't noticed her until right this second. Probably because her dyed red hair blended in so well with her flowers.

Crap. I didn't mean to get spotted. What do I do now? Run?

"You are, aren't you?" she asks when I don't answer.

I…"

She points her little gardening shovel at me. "Just what do you think you're doing here?"

Blair and I never got to the stage of our relationship where she introduced me to her parents. I'm not an idiot, though. I know she was embarrassed. I know she figured they would disapprove.

"You know, for being such a little lady, you are still pretty scary," I say.

This only seems to make Blair's mom madder.

"You broke Blair's heart," she tells me. "Do you have any idea how upset she is?"

"How did you know who I was?"

She huffs. "She showed me photos of you, of course. And I have one of those Instagram things, too. I know when she posts pictures. She was head-over-heels for you, and you crushed her. You should be ashamed of yourself."

"Well, maybe you should be thanking me." I shoot her a drunken smile. "Now, she can find somebody better. I mean, look at me. Do you think *I* would be good for her?"

"You *were* good for her. You were somebody who taught her how to let loose and have fun. She had always been so serious and focused on her future. You were the one who taught her to live in the present."

So, she did approve of me?

No, that can't be true.

"Trust me. You would *not* want someone like me as your son-in-law someday," I say. "I don't know the first thing about being a good boyfriend. I don't think I know the first thing about being a good person in general."

"Oh, I think you do," she argues. "You're just so worried that you were going to fail and let my daughter down that you made sure it happened. That way, if you let her down on purpose, you could control the situation and prevent yourself from getting hurt by her first."

I shrug. "Yeah, well, she'll get over me. She will find someone better."

"You are going to regret this for the rest of your life."

I can't let her words get to me. Instead, I smile.

"Well, I was just passing through. It was nice to finally meet you, Mrs. Cosgrove. You have an exceptional daughter." Then I give her a wave and carry on with my walk.

Someone barges into my room at my parents' house and snaps the lights on. "Brennan, get up! Derek's in jail."

My eyes snap open. The clock on my nightstand reads three in the morning. Dad's pulling on his jacket over his sleeping t-shirt, his white tennis shoes already on his feet.

I roll out of bed. "What happened?" I ask while I fumble around for something to quickly put on.

"I don't know, but you're coming with me to go get him."

I get dressed and meet Dad at his truck. He drives carelessly and recklessly on the icy road.

"Dad, slow down! Derek isn't going anywhere." I try. He's going to kill us before we can even get to the station.

"I just don't understand it," Dad says, shaking his head over and over. I wonder if we're finally thinking the same thing. That Derek hit Selena, and she finally called the cops about it.

When we get to the station, two officers, both my dad's age, greet us by the front desk.

"A bar downtown called it in," one of the officers explains. "He was acting drunk and disorderly. We're holding him in a cell, but don't worry. We didn't charge him with anything."

Dad hugs both of them, and I stand there itching my head, confused. But when I stare harder, I recognize the officers. They're friends of my father.

"How is he now?" I ask them, relieved that Derek wasn't arrested for a different reason.

"Still pretty drunk," the shorter one says.

"Pretty disorderly still, too, if we're being honest," the other one adds in.

Dad sighs. "Let's go."

We follow the two officers to the back, where Derek is pacing around in a cell that he has to himself. His knuckles are bloody, and he has a black eye.

An officer unlocks the cell and opens it.

"Come on, Derek, let's go," Dad says. Derek avoids

either of our gazes as he storms out. Dad and I race after him, Dad yelling a *thank you* at the cops over his shoulder as we go. Out in the parking lot, Derek punches a fist into his other hand and growls angrily.

"You know, I should kill her," he slurs.

"What?" I ask.

"Derek, get in the car," Dad demands.

"She ruined my life."

"Who did?" I challenge.

"Derek! Brennan! In the truck!"

Derek is still belligerently drunk. "Leah! She ruined my life with that interview. She is a nobody. She's just jealous that I am a *somebody*."

"Trust me, bro. Nobody wants to be you." It feels good to say it. While I'm at it, I also want to threaten him for threatening Leah, but he's drunk right now. If I'm going to talk to him, I want to make sure his sober ears hear me.

Dad grabs Derek and pulls him over to the backseat. I open the door for them, and Dad pushes him inside. Derek continues to yell angrily the entire drive home.

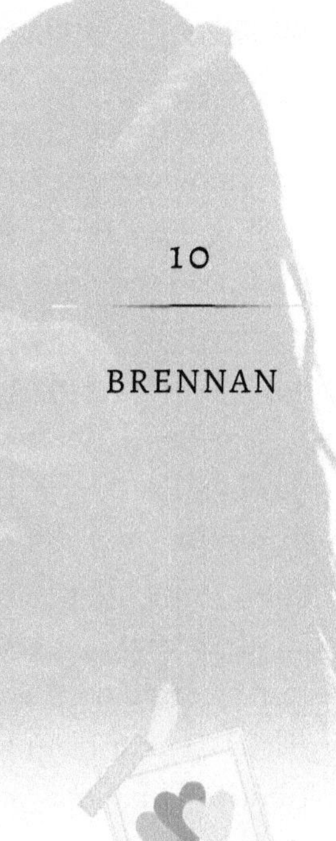

10

———

BRENNAN

The next morning, I wake up to a text from Leah.

Leah: *Do you want to meet me for coffee?*

Me: *Sounds good. Where am I going?*

She sends me the address of my cousin's coffee shop. I tell her to give me an hour so I can shower, get ready, and deal with any potential family drama.

When I get to the coffee shop, Leah is waiting for me outside in the cold.

I park my car and get out. "You okay?" I ask as I walk toward her.

Thankfully, she gives me a warm smile. "Yeah. Just figured I would wait out here and not hold up the line."

I sort of want to hug her, but it's not something we've done. So instead, I hold the door open for her, and we go inside. She orders a black coffee, and I get two shots of espresso. Jennifer isn't working this shift, but I'm not too mad about it because I don't want to have to explain to her later who Leah is.

"So," I start, drumming my fingers against the espresso cup as we sit at a small table.

She sips her coffee, then makes a face like it burned her tongue. "Thanks for meeting me," she says.

"Yeah, I was surprised to hear from you."

"Yeah I… I don't know. Um, so a lot of people have been messaging me on Instagram."

"Oh, yeah? About what?"

"About… Derek. Girls from high school. Other places, too. Some of them have told me their similar experiences. Some even said it was okay for me to pass their message along to Kenneth, that reporter guy. So, I suppose I should warn you that things might start getting a little worse for your brother."

I love how unafraid she is to tell me about it. How she doesn't seem to feel even the slightest bit guilty about breaking the news about getting my brother into trouble. She's a lot stronger and braver than she thinks she is.

"Good," I tell her. "The more, the better. You're inspiring them, Leah."

She smiles sheepishly and tucks some hair behind her ear. "It's a pretty nice feeling."

As nice as it is to see her again and have coffee together, I still don't really know why she invited me here. She can't actually want to be friends after all, can she? Not if she's going to see Derek every time she looks at me.

I sip my espresso and nod my head. "Well, I'm happy for you."

When she looks at me, there's a certain twinkle in her eye. "Yeah. Um, there was this one girl, Megan Clark. I don't know if you remember her. But she went to our high school. I actually ran into her at the grocery store."

"Oh, Megan? Yeah, she was a nice girl."

Leah nods her head in agreement. "Yeah. She gave me a ton of compliments. Then she told me that she could tell that Derek was always a piece of shit. But do you know what she also said? She told me *his brother* was the total opposite. That *Brennan was always such a good guy.*"

"You're not trying to set me up with her, are you?" I ask, only half-joking.

She smirks at me. "No. It just got me thinking. You have *always* been a good guy. I think everybody in Quincy knows that."

I nod slowly. "Glad you're starting to see it."

She smiles, and the way she looks down at her cup makes me realize she's nervous. "Yes. So, that brings me to my point. I'm sorry I didn't realize it on Valentine's Day when you brought me those beautiful flowers. But I want to go on a date with you. If… if that's something you'd be interested in."

I grin at her. "You know what? I think that *is* something I might have great, *great* interest in."

It's really happening. I'm going to take Leah Olson out on a date. The most beautiful and interesting woman in all of Quincy, and I get to take her out.

She smiles happily and bites her bottom lip as she looks at me. "Good, then." She sips some more. "But we would have to go slow. Like, probably excruciatingly slow."

I nod. "I can work with excruciatingly slow." It's going to be hard because I already want to lean over the table and kiss her right here, but I'm sure I can manage. I may have only hung out with Leah a handful of times, but I can already tell she's worth it.

11

———

GISELLE

*B*lair calls me right after I leave a hair appointment. I got a trim, highlights added, and a blowout. Now I'm feeling refreshed and beautiful again.

"B! What's up?" I ask when I answer.

"So, I did something crazy," Blair says.

I pause outside the door to my car. "Define *crazy*. In Blair terms," I tell her. Usually, my sister's idea of crazy is pulling an all-nighter on homework.

"I, um, I think it might be Giselle-level crazy."

I grin. "Oh my gosh, *what?* Did you have rebound sex?"

"Ew, no! I'm in LA!"

"I'm sorry, what?!"

"Yeah! I just… I don't know. I started looking at flights early this morning, then I just decided to get a ticket. Is that okay? Can I stay at your place?"

Excitement soars through me as I squeal and get in my car. "Are you kidding me? That's amazing! Tell me where you are. I'll come pick you up."

***

AFTER I BRING Blair to my penthouse and give her the grand tour, she wanders over to my fridge and pulls out a bottle of champagne. "This is all you have?"

I frown. "Well, we have the perfect reason to celebrate! Let's open it."

She rolls her eyes. "I was hoping for something stronger. We should go out tonight. I can finally see what it's like to legally party with my older sister!"

I know my sister is heartbroken over Damascus, but I didn't realize until now how bad it is. My sister is not the clubbing type. She has never once expressed excitement about the both of us being old enough to drink together. Nor did I ever think I'd hear her say she wanted something stronger than champagne.

"It's, like, the middle of the week," I say. "Wait a second. Don't you have school?"

She opens the bottle with ease and doesn't even jump when the cork pops loose. "Yeah, but who cares?"

"What the hell are you talking about?"

She shrugs. "Oh, stop. I'll be fine."

"Okay…" I think about questioning her further, but who am I to be the responsible one? Blair came to see me, after months and months of me begging her to do it. Now that she's here, I'm going to show her a good time.

I grin. "Well, you know what? Who cares if it's the middle of the week? I know some amazing spots we can hit up."

She digs around in my cupboards and finds herself two wine glasses. Then she pours us both a glass.

"To finding me some rebound sex!" she says when she clinks her glass to mine. I gasp at her boldness, but then I giggle, and we drink.

12

KENNETH

I've kept coming up with excuses to Rainer about why I can't come home yet. But with him threatening to stop paying my rent and my rental car, my excuses are running out.

I just feel weird about leaving Selena here with Derek. I know she *chose* to go back to him, but I can't help it; something doesn't feel right, and I want to try to see her one last time before I go.

It doesn't matter how many times my internal voice

is screaming at me that I'm being an idiot, I drive to Derek's house, anyway. I have a flight booked, and my bags packed in my trunk. My next stop after this place is finally back to LA.

When I pull up to the house, I reach a dilemma. Derek's gate is closed, and I highly doubt he will let me in himself. So, I drive a couple houses down and park on the street. Then I dive between some hedges, scratching the hell out of myself in the process, and climb over the fence that's surrounding the residence. When I jump and touch down on the other side, my ankles throb, but I shake it off and cut across the manicured grass. I don't pause once to think about what I will say if Derek is the one to answer the door, but I don't care. I will find a way. I have to make sure Selena is okay.

I obnoxiously ring the doorbell four times, and then pound on the door loudly. Sweat beads up on my forehead despite how cold it is outside.

Please be Selena who answers. Please be Selena who answers.

The door unlocks. It creaks open. My chest falls.

It's Derek. He is a little beat-up looking, too.

Good.

"What the hell do you want?" Derek asks.

"Is Selena here? I need to talk to her." I don't care if he had no idea that I've spent so much time with her since arriving in Quincy, and I don't care how much trouble he tries to make for me after he finds out.

"Why? Trying to see about interviewing her for your next made-up story about me?" Derek asks.

I can't help but laugh. "Right. *Made* up."

I don't know what I was expecting—maybe I

thought Derek and I would have a little bit more back-and-forth banter before anything really got out of hand. But when he swiftly reaches out and punches me in the jaw, I stagger back and grab onto one of his brick pillars for support. I had *not* been expecting that.

"Come back here again, and you're a dead man." Derek slams the door shut and locks it.

* * *

I suppose I should have expected it to go that way. My adrenaline and need to see Selena just took over my body, and I hadn't been thinking or seeing clearly.

So, it's done. I'm at the airport, about to board the plane and go back to LA. I probably won't have any reason to come back to Quincy for a long, long time. I'll never hear from Selena again, and I will never get to know what happened to her.

She hadn't come to the door. She hadn't called or texted me to reach out. I had to accept it. It didn't matter how I felt about her because Derek messed her up, and she was never going to become strong enough to leave him.

I get to fly in first class because my boss likes me again. I buckle myself in my seat and stare at my phone, telling myself not to go through the pictures that Selena and I had taken together inside my rental. Then when the plane is fully boarded and the doors close, I put my phone on airplane mode and put it away.

I take a sleeping aid, so I'm unconscious for nearly the entire flight home. I only wake up when the plane lands. Then I get nervous as I take my phone off airplane mode, like I am anticipating hearing bad news.

I step off the airplane and onto the jetway, discovering that I have a voicemail from Leah.

No one else.

I put my phone to my ear and listen to her message. "Hey, Kenneth. I just went to your house, but you weren't there, and it looked kind of empty through the windows. Not that I checked. Well, obviously, I did. But anyway. I have bad news. I don't know if you heard from Selena, but she messaged me a little bit ago and… Derek has been threatening her, Kenneth. He's been saying awful stuff. Like he will kill her if she tries to leave him, or if she gives anyone a statement about him. I'm worried, and I don't know how to help. Call me when you get this."

My phone drops from my hand and falls to the floor.

13

DAMASCUS

*I*t's not that I'm obsessively checking or anything, but when the day rolls around that Blair has finally unblocked me on Instagram, I find myself checking it repeatedly. I'm not following her on the social media platform anymore, but I can tell on her page that she has something posted on her Instagram story, and I badly want to know what it is.

"I'm telling you," Andrew says to me. We're sitting on the couch in our apartment playing video games.

"She probably only unblocked you because she *wants* you to watch it. It's going to be her and some new dude or something."

"I'd be happy for her, if it were," I say. "She deserves to be happy."

Andy makes a gagging noise. "You're clearly still in love with her," he says. "So, what are you still doing with Jennifer?"

"No. You and Sara *wish* I were still in love with Blair. Because you don't like Jennifer."

"She's a bit—she's not a very nice girl. Of course, we don't like her. *She* didn't have to spend six months watching you destroy yourself."

"I'm gonna do it," I decide out of nowhere, referring to watching Blair's story.

Andrew shakes his head and gets another kill on the game. "Whatever, man." He's not very reassuring, but I click on it anyway. Blair's story is from last night. She's in LA, apparently. At nightclubs. Dressed in super short dresses and hanging out with celebrities.

"She's with her sister."

"Giselle Cosgrove? She's in Quincy again?"

I shake my head. "No, she's in LA, with Blair."

Andrew looks confused. "Doesn't Blair have school?"

My stomach sinks as I watch her story over and over and over. Blair doesn't look like a girl who cares about school in any of these photos. And in one of her videos, I think I recognize an actor from a teen drama show on TV.

"I thought so. But I guess I don't really know anymore."

Our front door opens, and Sara walks inside. "Um, just so you guys know, there is a creepy black car just sitting outside the apartment downstairs. There's a creepy guy inside, too. He's just been sitting there watching the building. I'm not saying it's our apartment —sorry—*your* guys' apartment, but it's definitely creepy."

I get up and race out the front door to lean over the railing and see what she's talking about. I'm just in time to watch as a man in a blacked-out car with heavily tinted windows rolls up his driver's window and peels away.

I go back inside, dread feeling me. "I think I know who that was," I tell them. "The governor is having me followed again."

14

BRENNAN

I am driving to my shop with Leah in my passenger seat. I picked her up because she told me that she wants to check it out. She's not particularly interested in sports, but she has always loved the idea of playing tennis. I told her we could buy some racquets and balls, and head to the park soon to try it out. I like any sports. And I like doing anything that involves hanging out with Leah.

"Oh my gosh, Brennan!" Leah screams, causing me

to slam on my brakes and send us both flying forward. I pull off to the side of the road in a panic.

"What's going on?!" I ask, turning to her. She's staring at her phone screen.

"Sorry. I didn't mean to make you almost kill us both. But it's Selena. She… she just messaged me and told me that Derek's threatening to kill her if she leaves their house. She doesn't know what to do, and she's scared to call the police."

I think about when we picked Derek up from jail the other night. How he had threatened to kill Leah, too. If he was willing to hit other women, how far was he actually willing to go? What exactly is my brother capable of?

Suddenly, I'm finding it hard to swallow. "Brennan?" Leah asks. She puts a hand on my shoulder. "I think she needs help. I'm calling Kenneth." She dials his number, and when he doesn't answer, she leaves him a voicemail.

"How long ago did she send you that message?" I ask her as she places her phone in my cupholder.

"Just now."

I put the car in park. Around us, other vehicles beep as they struggle to pass because I'm still partially in the road. Right now, I don't care.

"Leah, I need you to get out of the car."

"What, why?"

"I'm going over there."

"Brennan, no. That's a bad idea."

"Leah. Please. There isn't time to discuss this right now. You don't understand. You have to get out of the car."

"N-no," she tries. "No, I'm going with you."

I shake my head. "No, you're not."

Leah looks scared. "We should just call the police and let them go over there or something," she says. "Brennan, please don't do this."

"I'll be fine, Leah. He's my brother. It's going to be okay. I'm just gonna go talk to him."

Still, she doesn't move. "Just let me come. I will stay in the truck, even. Please? I'll feel better knowing that you're okay."

"And I'll feel better knowing that *you're* okay. So, no. You have to get out of my car." I'm doing everything in my power not to say anything that will scare or upset her. I'm not raising my voice. I'm not threatening to drag her out myself. But if she doesn't get out, I'm afraid I might start.

Leah glares at me. "This is so stupid." She unbuckles her seatbelt, opens the truck door, and hops out.

I drive away quickly before she can try and get back in. I can't risk her getting hurt, too.

When I get to the gate outside my brother's house, I unroll the window and punch in the code to open it. The second I park the car and get out, I can hear Selena screaming inside. Scared out of my mind, I run up to the front door. It's locked. Selena is still screaming inside. Derek is yelling.

I hop off the porch, grab a large rock from their front landscape, and go back to the door. I smash the rock into the glass pane and shatter it. Then I reach through and unlock it from the inside. I hope the sound was loud enough that Derek stops whatever he's doing to Selena and comes to find me.

I step inside their foyer, panting heavily. "Derek! Selena! Where are you?!"

Selena screams some more, then it is abruptly cut off.

Trying not to think about what my brother might've done to shut her up, I race toward the west side of the house, where I heard them before.

"Derek! Come here!" I shout. But it's completely silent now. I enter room after room, searching for them frantically.

Please let her be alive. Please let her be alive.

I try their master bedroom door, but it's locked. Using all the strength I have, I kick it open. I don't care if I have to burn this entire house down to get to Selena. I will do it.

Their master bedroom, which is about as big as the entire second floor of my parents' house, is empty. But somewhere off in their en suite bathroom, I hear a muffled cry.

I respond. "Derek! Where are you?! Come on, dude. I just want to talk!" I walk into the bathroom. Over in their master closet, I hear the crying grow louder. I open the door, and there Selena is, tied up on the floor with tape over her mouth. She's trying to say something to me as I rush forward, but I don't know what it is. The first thing I do is rip the tape off her mouth.

"Selena, oh my gosh. Are you—"

"Behind you!" she screams.

I turn around just as Derek lunges at me. I fly into a

closet shelf, clothes toppling down on top of me. Derek punches me in the face. I instinctively bring my knee up to hit him in the stomach. He flies away from me and into the opposite shelf.

"Derek, stop!" I try. He punches me again, and as I taste blood in my mouth, he grabs me by my collar and drags me out of the closet. "Derek, stop!" Selena screams from inside, still tied up and unable to help.

"Shut up!" Derek shouts at her as he punches me again, this time, right in the diaphragm. I double over, and he knocks me to the ground. There, he kicks me several times. Looking all around me, I don't see anything to grab onto. So, I reach for his foot as it comes at me again and twist as hard as I can. He falls to the ground, but lands on top of me. I cry out in pain at his crushing weight on my injuries and try to get him off, but he scrambles wildly and manages to pin me down.

In the background, Selena continues to scream and cry and beg for him to stop. "He's your brother!" she shouts.

But Derek's fist keeps slamming into my face. Over and over and over, until I stop feeling anything at all. Selena's screams start fading away, and everything around me turns black.

15

GISELLE

I am with Blair at a late brunch when Eliza calls my cell. I smile at my sister. "This is Eliza," I say to her. "The one I told you about." I didn't tell Blair anything about my feelings for her, of course. I just mentioned how close of a friend she was, and about how her husband is sick.

Blair gives me a thumbs up, shoveling eggs and bacon into her mouth.

I answer the call. "Good morning," I say in a

chipper mood. Having Blair hang out with me has been a total blast. Even if she shouldn't be avoiding school.

"Giselle, I have some news; do you have a second?"

My stomach dips, and I stand from the table. I mouth to Blair that I will be right back, then I leave the restaurant and step outside into the sun. "Yeah, what's going on?"

"Shawn asked if we could sell the house."

"The one you just bought?" I ask.

"Well, it's been nearly a year…"

"Wow. Okay." Is she calling to see if I have a good realtor?

"I told him yes, and he was able to sell it within twenty-four hours. Giselle, he wants to spend the remainder of his life back in Quincy."

It feels like a knife has just been stabbed through my chest. "And you're going with him?"

She sighs. "I know it's not a practical place to be a fashion designer, but right now, I have to do that. You can understand that, right?"

Of course, I understand, but that doesn't mean it's easy. "Oh… Yes, Liza. Of course. Go be with your husband in Quincy."

"Ugh, Giselle, you are always so understanding. Thank you." We talk a little bit longer, then hang up. I am completely heartbroken and feel like my world has just shifted, but I have to go back to my sister and pretend like I'm completely fine.

I'm terrified about doing so because I know I can't act.

16

DAMASCUS

I figure a drive around in my truck with the windows down and some rock music playing is just what I need in order to think. It's the perfect place for me to ponder my relationship with Jennifer. And what I am pondering about right now, is that it's just not working with her.

I don't know really how to explain it, but things are just different with her. With me. I don't like who I am with her. I don't like the old patterns we fell back into.

And she keeps trying to act like nothing ever changed, but it did. In a huge way.

I just don't know if I can do it.

As I drive, I squint at the strange woman sprinting down the sidewalk in jeans and an oversized sweater. Then as I get nearer, I realize I *know* this woman. I drive a little bit ahead of her and slam on my brakes. "Leah?!" I yell at her out my window.

"Damascus!" she cries in relief. Then without another word, she runs to my passenger side and climbs in. "Drive me to the police station!" She is sweating and panting, and her eyes look wild.

"Are you okay?" I try asking first.

She shoves me a little bit. "Drive!"

Terrified, I do as she asks. "I'm going! What the hell is going on?"

"I left my phone in Brennan's truck!"

"Okay, do you want mine?"

She hits me again. "Don't stop at the stop sign; just drive!"

I take my foot off the brake and hit the gas again, nearly colliding with an old woman driver who is following the law and going when she's supposed to.

"How far away are we?" Leah demands.

"Leah, it's going to be oka—"

"*How far away are we?!*"

Her voice is so shrill that it startles me, and I nearly swerve into the other lane and hit another car. She is going to get us both killed talking to me like this.

I point straight. "It's right up there!" I yell at her.

She taps her foot anxiously as we approach the

station. I barely even put my truck in park before she is climbing out of it and racing inside. I rush in after her, not about to leave her alone at a time like this.

She goes to the nearest officer. "You have to help!" she shouts. Then I listen as she explains to the cops how she thinks Derek Heed's wife is in danger, along with his younger brother, Brennan. Apparently, Derek Heed has been threatening to kill his wife. And Brennan, trying to be brave, kicked Leah out of his car and drove over there to go interfere himself.

The officers tell us to wait here, then some of them take off.

Leah looks at me. "You don't happen to have Brennan Heed's phone number, do you?"

I shake my head at her, feeling distressed. Then after practically having to force her, I get her to sit down and hand her a cup of bad vending machine coffee.

"I should've gone with," Leah says over and over while still tapping her anxious foot. "I have a horrible feeling right now. Call it a woman's intuition or whatever. But something isn't right."

I take her hand and hold it tightly. "We just have to wait and see, okay? Try to push the negative thoughts aside until you know for certain."

She squeezes my hand back and puts her head on my shoulder.

We wait.

When one of the officers finally gets back, Leah flies out of her chair.

Now, even *I* am a little nervous to hear this news, and I don't even know who these people are.

"We got to them," one of the officers says. "Just in time, too."

"What does that mean?!" Leah screeches. I am pretty sure she must be in love with this Brennan guy or something.

"Brennan Heed was in pretty bad shape. He's at the hospital now."

Leah lets out a strangled cry and runs past him and out of the building. "Damascus! Come on!" she shouts over her shoulder.

I brace myself for another terrifying car ride to the hospital.

17

KENNETH

$\mathcal{I}$ call Selena's phone probably a hundred times. Not once does she answer. Not once does it go straight to voicemail, though. It's not dead. It's like she just lets it keep ringing. It has to mean that Selena isn't by her phone, which only stresses me out more; Selena is always by her phone.

I haven't even left the airport yet. I'm sitting at the gate that I walked out of, feeling horrible about coming back here in the first place. I should've known something was wrong. I should have tried harder to get to Selena when I had the chance.

Selena doesn't answer again when I call, and neither does Leah when I try her.

I can't help it. I stand up from my chair.

"Damn it!" I bellow. Then I run my hands through my hair, not knowing what else I can possibly do.

And when I see everyone staring at me, I wave at them in apology, then I walk off and try both women again. Nothing.

If Derek kills her, then it's on me.

Thinking quickly, I search for Giselle's contact and give her a call next.

18

GISELLE

’m currently sitting in a private jet with my sister, Eliza, and Kenneth. When Kenneth called me in desperation not long ago, he had informed me that he somehow knew about me and Eliza. Then he asked for help to get a private jet so he could go back to Quincy. He didn’t outright threaten me, but it felt like I didn’t have a choice, regardless. I told Eliza about it, and she decided to come with me at a moment’s notice.

Toward the back of the plane, Blair and I are sitting

on a couch next to each other. Toward the front, Kenneth and Eliza are speaking to each other in hushed tones.

"Why are we helping them?" Blair asks me quietly. I'm feeling crummy right now over the news about Eliza leaving me, and the fact that her stepson knows about us. I'm not trying to take it out on my sister, but the words come out of my mouth anyway.

"You need to go home," I tell her. "You need to finish school and get your degree, Blair."

She looks upset. "I thought we were having fun together."

"We were! And we will continue to have fun some other time! But you can't let a stupid boy be the reason you didn't go after your dream. Besides, with my dream, it can only last so long. My beauty is going to fade one day. Your brains will last a lifetime."

"Wow. That has to be, like, the most adult thing I've ever heard you say."

I throw my arm around her and hug her close to me.

Maybe I am slowly finally learning how to become one.

19

DAMASCUS

waited with Leah inside the hospital for as long as I could stand, but truth be told, I don't normally do hospitals. So, after a while, I head out front and sit on top of a short pillar attached to the steps. I'm not going to leave her here, so I told her I'd be waiting if she needs anything.

About forty-five minutes pass before Leah comes outside. "Brennan is okay. So is Selena," she informs me.

I am relieved—mainly for *her* sake. I know all too well how much it sucks to lose someone you care about.

I hop off the pillar and smile at her. "Good. Are *you*?"

Leah's eyes are bloodshot, her hair is a tangled mess, and she has circles under her eyes. I can tell she's exhausted. "Yeah. Damascus, thank you so much for helping me. If it had taken me any longer to get to the police station…"

I nudge her. "Hey, you don't have to think like that. It's okay."

She nods her head in agreement.

I look up and see a familiar black car off in the distance. It's the same one that had been outside of my apartment building before. I'm sure of it now. I am being followed again.

This PI is probably getting pictures of me standing with Leah right now. I am going to have to explain myself to Jennifer all over again when she sees the new photos of us.

And as I'm standing here now, I'm realizing that I really don't feel like doing that. I don't want to explain myself to Jennifer ever again.

I look at Leah standing next to me. I never even told her about how Jennifer thought I was cheating on her with her. So, it was going to make it extra confusing when I do what I am about to do, but it doesn't matter. I can explain it to Leah after.

With the car still watching me, I grab Leah's face and pull her into me, then I kiss her right on the lips, long and hard so that the investigator can get a really good photo, even though Leah is struggling against me.

When I pull away, I grin at her. "Let me tell you why I just did that," I say. But before I can get another word out, Leah's face twists into anger, and she unexpectedly punches me in the face.

20

KENNETH

As soon as we touch back down in Quincy, the four of us—Giselle, her sister, Eliza, and I—race to the hospital after a news article online had already posted about the gruesome fight at Derek Heed's house between him, Selena, and Brennan.

When we get there, I learn quickly from Leah, whose phone is in Brennan's truck, that Selena is okay. She's in observation and talking with the police now.

Relieved, but desperate to see Selena, I head to the waiting room and take a seat next to Eliza.

"They're okay," I say with a sigh. Eliza nods at me. Now that I know Selena isn't dead, I can think more clearly about the other people around me. About the fact that I know my stepmother and Giselle have a thing for each other.

"Kenneth," Eliza starts, looking around to see if we're going to be overheard. When she sees that we're not, she continues. "About Giselle…"

"I'm not going to say anything," I admit. "As weird as this sounds, I don't actually care. I just wanted to ensure that Giselle would help me. I needed to get to Selena. You'll apologize to her for me, right?"

Eliza nods but still looks like there's more she wants to stay. "I… I know this is bad timing right now, Kenny. But your father and I are moving here. *Back* here."

When she sees my surprise, she launches into her explanation. In the end, I agree. Being in Quincy will be the best place for my dad to live the remainder of his life.

Shortly after our discussion, Giselle approaches us with her sister in tow. "I'm going to drop her off at home," Giselle says. "Then I guess I'm heading back to LA."

Eliza goes to stand, but Giselle quickly moves away.

"I'm glad they're okay," she continues. "I hope you guys get a safe flight home." There are tears in her eyes as she gives my stepmom one final look.

I'm guessing that she's already heard the news about Eliza moving away from her.

"Take care of yourself," Eliza says. Giselle nods, and she and Blair leave the building.

21

BRENNAN

"It's not as bad as it looks," I tell Selena inside the hospital room as I lie in my bed. She is standing before me with her arms crossed, shaking her head, her bruised arms and scratched face nothing to compare to my appearance.

"Why did you do that, Brennan?"

"Do what, Selena?" It also helps that I am on quite a bit of pain medication.

"You have proven your point," she says. "I get that

you're sorry. You don't have to keep trying to repay me for when you didn't believe me when I told you about Derek the first time." She looks half-sad and half-pleased. I'm not quite sure which expression to believe. But I do feel like I did the right thing still.

"I feel responsible because he's my brother," I tell her. "It doesn't have anything to do with owing you." We stare at each other for a bit, and then I crack a smile even though it hurts my face. "Okay, it doesn't have *everything* to do with you," I admit.

She smiles and shakes her head, and then before I can say another word, Leah breezes in through the open door. She looks frazzled and conflicted about something as she walks over to my bedside. I'm happy to see her, and even happier when she leans down to give me a hug. But instead of hugging me, she kisses me right on the lips. Right on my bruised, cut, and swollen lips.

But it doesn't hurt one bit.

This is the first time it has happened. I hadn't yet made the move to kiss Leah, regardless of how many times we have hung out. She said she wanted to take it slow, so I had always been respectful of that.

When Leah pulls away from our first kiss, she smiles at me and strokes my face gently.

"If I had known you were going to kiss me, I would have gotten myself beat up ages ago," I joke. I want to laugh, but it hurts.

Leah does, though.

"So… I—um, Damascus just kissed me," she tells me after. "That little jerk just kissed me! Can you believe it?"

I don't know Damascus that well, but I don't like the sound of this. "He *did?*" I ask. "Are you okay?" I know how scared of being touched Leah is. What the hell was that kid thinking?

"Oh, great, *another* guy Brennan has to go beat up," Selena says.

Leah stands up straight and shakes her head, still looking in a daze. "No, no. I'm not mad. It's fine. He's just got… got some problems he's dealing with. I'm actually kind of surprised that I'm not *madder*. I mean… I haven't kissed anybody in… a long time."

"And now you've kissed two in what—three minutes?" Selena jokes. I chuckle in my bed. I like Selena. I wish I had given myself the chance to get to know her much sooner than I did.

Leah turns and smiles at Selena. "I am so glad you guys are okay." The two of them exchange a hug. They have been messaging back and forth on social media and over text for a while now, but I'm not actually sure if they have ever hung out in person before.

Then, as I lie there and watch them catch up, in walks Leah's *parents*, of all people.

"Mom? Dad?" Leah asks, stepping around Selena to go talk to them. "What are you doing here?"

They look at me. "Hey, Brennan. How are you holding up?"

"Pretty good," I answer. But for some reason, Leah's dad's face still looks grim.

"I have news."

"What is it?" Leah asks.

Already, our romantic moment seems like years ago.

"I don't know if we already told you, Brennan. But I have a law background," her father says. "And I know about the ones that Derek Heed has just landed himself. They're good. Extremely good."

"What does that mean?" Selena asks. Even though she is a little bruised and cut up, too—again, nothing compared to how I look—she isn't in a hospital bed of her own.

"It means that if you try to press charges, you most likely won't win," Leah's mom clarifies.

Selena turns to look at me. I don't really know what to say.

"What?" Leah asks instead of either of us. "You don't think they should press charges against Derek?"

"I'm just saying that it's risky," her dad replies. "I know it's not what you want to hear. And I'm not telling you both what to do; I just thought you should know."

All three of us are probably thinking the same thing; how is Derek supposed to get what he deserves if nobody does anything to stop him?

22

DAMASCUS

Some time has passed since that day at the hospital when those Brennan and Selena people were attacked by that football player, Derek Heed. I kissed Leah outside the hospital because I knew that the governor was having me followed, and I knew his private investigator would get photos of me kissing her. And I knew he would show them to Jennifer.

It didn't even take her an entire day to chase me down, smack me a hundred times in my chest and once across the face, and then she dumped me again. I told her I couldn't help it, that I had no way to make myself stay away from Leah.

I don't know why I lied, and why I didn't just outright tell her that I don't want to be with her anymore. I think making sure she couldn't trust me anymore was the best way to do it. That way, she won't try to come back to me ever again.

But now, I need to go after what it is I *really* want. I've decided to stop sitting around feeling sorry for myself. "Self-sabotaging" as other people have been saying.

According to Blair's Instagram story, she is at the college, in the library, sitting at her favorite cubicle and studying for an upcoming test. So, I know just where to find her.

Dressed in all black with my hands in my pockets and a determined expression on my face, I know I don't fit in at the library. Every person I walk past stares at me, wondering what I'm up to. But I don't care. My thoughts are on Blair and Blair only.

My heart stops when I find her. Her head is down as she works diligently. She's wearing a giant hoodie, her hair is in a messy bun, she has on no makeup, and is wearing her blue-light computer glasses.

I think she looks perfect.

I sit down next to her at the next study cubicle. At first, she doesn't look up—she probably assumes I am just another student coming to cram. So, then I adjust my seat and scoot closer to her so that I can see all the way inside of her cubicle.

She turns her head, looking ready to tell off whoever is bothering her, and then when she sees that it's me, she jumps in her chair and nearly falls off of it.

"Damascus!" she hisses quietly. "What the hell are you doing here?"

She immediately fixes her hair and smooths out her hoodie, and I know she's embarrassed that I caught her dressed like this. I wish she knew how beautiful I still think she is.

"I need to tell you something," I say.

She lets out a long breath. "Damascus, I can't do this."

I lick my lips. "Please, Blair. It's something I should've told you while we were still together."

"I'm trying to study for a big test. I know you know that because I saw that you watched my story. Which is weird, considering that you're not even following me on Instagram."

"Blair, my brother died."

Her mouth hangs open like she had been about to tell me to go away, but suddenly doesn't want to anymore.

I continue, my heart racing, just wanting to get this over with. I never talk about my brother. Or my family. Or anything about my past, really. And that's not fair to her. How can I have a relationship with somebody who knows nothing about me? About why I am the way that I am?

"My brother had ALS. I lived with him because my parents died in a car crash when I was younger. He was only in his twenties. It happened two years ago. It was fast and sudden, and there was nothing I could do about it. Out of nowhere, I was on my own."

She looks heartbroken for me. "Damascus, I had no idea."

I nod. "I know. Because I didn't tell you. I don't tell anyone, ever. I go to a support group for it. It's for people who have ALS and their families. Leah runs the support group."

Her eyebrows furrow together. For some reason, she looks like she's about to cry.

"I'm really damaged, Blair. I've been through a lot of stuff in my life. And I act out because of it. And I felt like that wasn't fair to you. Blair, it was Jennifer who kissed me that day out at the waterfront. I didn't stop her because I thought maybe I wasn't meant to be with somebody as good as you. I thought I weighed you down. For a long while, I thought it was better if I just stayed with her. But that wasn't the case. And I've been an idiot."

"Damascus…" she trails off, setting her glasses down on her desk and turning toward me. Whatever she is about to tell me right now is going to determine where our future is heading. I just know it.

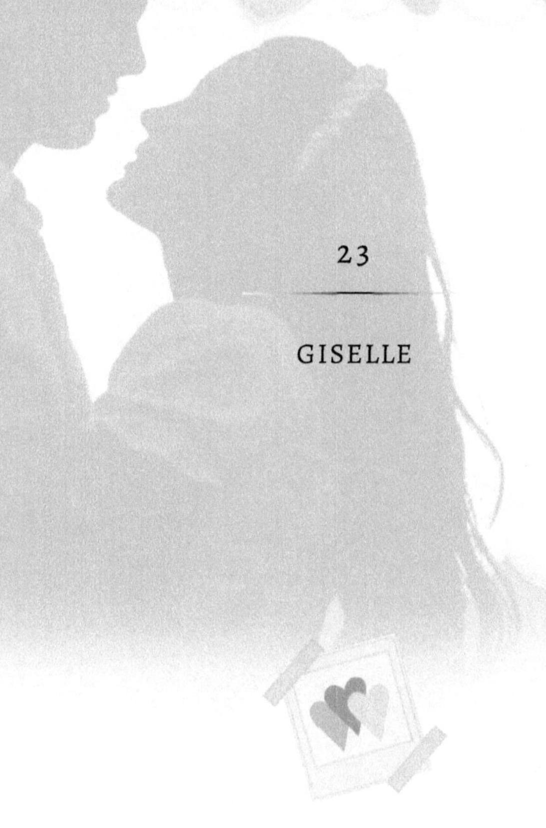

23

GISELLE

I've been back in LA and without Eliza for a couple of weeks now. All I can really say about it is that it sucks.

I really miss her.

24

KENNETH

I'm back in LA.

After I raced back to Quincy to make sure Selena was okay when I heard that Derek attacked her, we talked and even hugged. She admitted to me that Derek had found her at the New Year's Eve party and demanded she come home with him. She had been held at their house against her will. While it made me feel horrible because I wished I had just been smart enough to know what had happened to her, the tiniest bit of me was relieved. We had been in a fight that night, but it hadn't been the reason that she left.

Still, I had to return to LA. Rainer was calling me back to work at the main office, and I didn't know what Selena's plans were for her upcoming future. Part of me felt as if she were still going to stay with Derek, anyway. That she still wasn't strong enough to be done with it. Especially after I learned recently that both Brennan and Selena decided not to press charges.

I'm sitting at my desk at my place, working on an article about Lindsay Barr, a celebrity who was spotted cheating on her husband. It surprisingly doesn't seem nearly as exciting of a story as Derek Heed's had been.

I am interrupted from my work by a knock on the door.

I don't get many unannounced visitors, so I assumed it was my sister, Eliza, a mailman, or maybe even… my dad?

The last person I expected it to be was Selena, but when I open the door and see her standing there, her long blonde hair pulled back and her face smiling wildly at me, I almost don't believe it.

"I come bearing gifts?" Selena asks outside my door. Still shocked, I step aside and let her in, speechless.

"You okay ?" she asks after she enters.

I close the door and nod. Then I finally clear my throat. "Selena. This is… a surprise." Am I dreaming? I *must* be dreaming. Or hallucinating. Did I accidentally take some drugs that I don't know about?

She nods her head slowly and looks around my place. She's been here before, from when we had

Christmas together, but it's a lot messier now than it had been back then. I've been too bummed out to really feel like doing any chores lately.

"I'm so sorry to barge in on you like this," she begins. "I just wasn't sure how you would react if I called you first, so I decided to just show up at your doorstep instead."

"In typical Selena fashion," I joke. She had shown up randomly at my doorstep in Quincy, too. At least, she doesn't have a black eye this time.

She giggles. Then she reaches in her purse and pulls out a folder. When she hands it to me, our fingers graze. I can't believe how one simple touch can make me realize how much I've missed her.

"As far as everyone knows, these don't exist," she tells me. "I said I had gotten rid of all the evidence of what Derek did to me and Brennan. But I didn't."

I open the file and don't believe my eyes. It's photos of Derek attacking her and Brennan at his house. They are screenshots from their security cameras. Then after those, there are photos of Selena. Of her injuries. They date all the way back to when they first got married.

"I documented it every time, from the very beginning," she explains. "Just because somewhere in my gut, I knew I would need this proof. I had a feeling things would go south in our relationship."

I open and close my mouth like a fish. "I—I don't understand," I manage to get out.

She adjusts the strap of her bag on her shoulder and continues smiling confidently. "They're for you to use. I am ready to give my statement. If you still want it."

I raise my eyebrows at her. "You…" I trail off. "What about Derek?" I haven't heard what he's been up to since he attacked his brother and his wife, but I don't like the idea of Selena living in the same town as him after letting me write an article about her experience. I don't want to get her in any sort of trouble again.

"Kenneth… I left him," she says. "It actually is going to be finalized pretty soon, but… we are getting a divorce."

25

BRENNAN

Even though the great Shawn Geiger can only talk to me using his ALS eye-movement-controlled computerized chair, it's incredible to meet him. Not only because he is a famous artist, but because Leah has spoken so highly of him. We're at his new house in Quincy, a big modern A-frame cabin home that's a short drive into the woods up a hill, off the beaten path. I'm not sure I even realized they had houses this big out here. And I don't know where he got all of the fancy furniture to put in it, either. It has to be the nicest house I have ever been inside of.

"You must be pretty special if Leah is willing to date you," Shawn says to me. Leah puts her arm around me and squeezes me close to her, placing her hand on my chest. It warms me up inside.

"I don't know about that," I reply, looking at her and smiling affectionately. Lately, we've seen each other every single day. I can't get enough of her.

"You're not planning on hurting her, are you?" Shawn asks. "Because if so, I'm afraid I'll have to kick your ass."

Leah and I laugh, and I can see a glimmer of a smile on Shawn's face.

"Thank you for having us over, Shawn," Leah tells him. "I'm so happy that you are back. And your house is lovely."

"Happy you came. And I'm happy that you found somebody," he says. "Don't ever forget, Leah. You deserve happiness."

She squints at him. "Using my own words against me, huh?"

Shawn looks back at me. "Brennan, keep her close to you."

I squeeze her tighter to my side. After everything that went down with me and Selena, I don't want to let Leah out of my sight. "Don't worry, Shawn. I plan on it."

26

KENNETH

I don't want Selena to go. I knew it the second she came to see me. I knew it the entire time I talked with her about Derek, and the entire day we spent together afterward. I knew it when we went out to a restaurant for dinner, and when we headed to a bar after for a couple of drinks. And now, as I stand here in the airport, taking her to security, I am more painfully certain of it than ever. I'm crazy about Selena.

"Well, I guess this is where I leave you," Selena tells me as we approach the security gate.

Part of me wants to buy a plane ticket just so I can walk through to the other side with her and wait with her until she boards. Another part of me wants to tell her not to go through security at all. But then *another* part of me is telling me to let her go. Why would she want to stay here in LA with me? Why am I even thinking it could be possible for her to feel anything for me at all? She just got out of a horrible relationship. I highly doubt she's going to want to enter into another one with *me*.

I bounce on the balls of my feet with my hands in my pocket as I look at Selena. "I guess so."

"Thank you again for everything you've done for me over the past… has it already been almost a year?" she asks. Spring is just around the corner.

"I guess so."

She smirks. "Funny how time flies when you're getting tormented by your future ex-husband."

I laugh, despite how morbid her comment is. Then I grab her shoulders. "I am really glad you came," I tell her as I stare deeply into her eyes.

Just tell me you want to stay here with me, I think to myself.

She smiles up at me. "Me, too."

Come on, Kenneth. Tell her how you feel.

Instead of saying anything, I pull her in for a long hug. She squeezes me back and buries her head in my chest. How badly I wish we could just stay like this.

Unfortunately, she steps away first. "I really should go," she says with a sigh.

I nod. "Alright, then. Have a safe flight."

"You, too," she says quickly. Then she shakes her head and blushes.

I chuckle.

"I mean… you know what I meant," she corrects. Then she turns and heads toward the security entrance. I turn to leave, too. But this is my only chance. This is the last opportunity I have to tell Selena that I don't want her to go.

Taking a deep breath in, I turn back around to her. "Selena!"

She stops and turns back to me. Her eyes are lit up in question as she smiles.

My stomach sinks. "Keep in touch," I say.

She hesitates for a moment, then she slowly gives me a thumbs up. "Okay… Will do." Then we turn and head in opposite directions.

I am a coward.

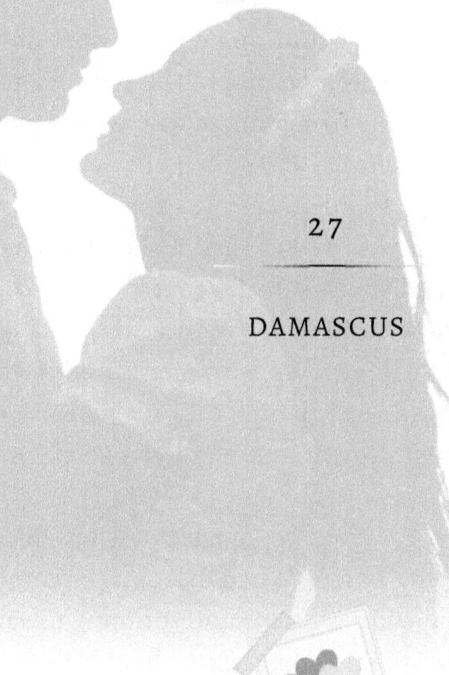

27

DAMASCUS

I leave the library with my head down. As I will myself to walk down the steps, I wonder how bad it would hurt if I just tripped myself and fell down them instead. At least the pain would be a nice distraction from how I'm feeling right now mentally.

I had laid it all out on the line for Blair. I told her everything about me. About my past. About feeling alone and going to therapy.

For the first time in my life, I have been one hundred

percent completely honest and vulnerable with somebody, and all it got me was a heartbreak all over again. I was shot down by the one woman in my life who is more important to me than anyone else.

It's a pretty crappy feeling.

As I walk to my truck, I wonder if I should go pick myself up some Jack Daniels. Or if I should go to a bar to drown my sorrows. But I don't want to do that. Just because Blair doesn't want to be with me, doesn't mean I have to be who I was with Jennifer. Blair changed me for the better, and with or without her, I can keep being better, right?

I open my truck door and get one leg in when I hear someone shouting my name. When I look up, there is Blair, racing down the library steps and sprinting toward me. I get back out of the truck and close the door.

What is she doing? I wonder to myself.

I start heading in her direction. She keeps running. So fast that I think she might knock me over. Instead, she jumps up and wraps her legs around me, and I catch her easily—she still weighs as much as a fourth-grader. Then she grips the sides of my face with both of her hands and presses her lips to mine.

Not once in my entire life have I felt so happy.

When she breaks away, her eyes are tearful. "I don't know what I was thinking," she says as I continue to hold her. "I love you, Damascus. More than anything in the entire world. And I want to make this work. I want to be with you."

Blair Cosgrove is in love with me.

I kiss her again and twirl her around, feeling like I

could fly away right now. I wish the two of us could. I wish we could just fly off into the sky and live in our own little world together. I wish that nothing would ever come between us again.

"You have no idea how happy I am to hear you say that," I tell her honestly. I like this whole "being honest" stuff. It makes me feel good inside. It makes me feel, finally, like I'm being myself. I'm being myself, and Blair still loves me.

How fucking crazy is that?

28

BRENNAN

As I drive to drop Leah back off at her place, she is all smiles. "What are you so happy about?" I ask. But I am feeling smiley, too. I had a wonderful time at Shawn's house with her. Shawn and Eliza are lovely people, and I hope I get to know Shawn more before the ALS overpowers him, and he is no longer with us.

Leah bobs her head to the alternative rock music I have playing on my radio. "It was just a really good night," she says as she looks at me.

I side-glance at her while driving. "It was, wasn't it?"

Then I gently place a hand on her knee. "Thank you for taking me to meet him," I say. I look down at my hand on her leg. "Is this okay?" I'm very respectful when it comes to placing my hands on her. The only things I know I can do for certain without asking are pecking her gently on the lips or hugging her.

She puts her hand on top of mine. "More than okay, actually." She squeezes my hand, so I squeeze her knee. Staring at it, she bites her bottom lip. "Brennan?"

"Yeah?"

"Will you come inside?"

I almost slam on my brakes. "Inside? As in… inside your house?"

She nods her head slowly, still biting her lip. It's so sexy that I nearly die inside.

"I understand if you don't want to," she continues. "I know the last time you did wasn't very… successful."

I laugh at the memory. How in the world did I go from getting tossed out her front door, with my shirt barely even on, to dating Leah? To having her wanting me back in her house? I never thought I would ever be stepping foot in there ever again. At least, not before I started dating her.

Don't get me wrong—I still hoped.

"Of course, I want to," I tell her. Then I take my hand off of her knee so that I can stroke her cheek with my thumb. She leans into my hand, looking at me through her lashes.

When I pull into her neighborhood and park on the

street in front of her small two-bedroom place, Leah leans over the middle console and kisses me. This time, it's more intense than any of the others we've had before. She's gripping my hair and stroking my back. Then suddenly, she climbs over so that she is straddling my lap.

I kiss her for a while, but eventually have to pull away, feeling breathless.

"Are you sure this is okay?" I ask. I don't want her to do anything she might potentially regret.

She rolls her eyes. "Shut up and kiss me."

I listen to her demands and dive back into her lips. I can't get enough of her.

Eventually, she opens my door, and we climb out. Then she takes my hand and pulls me all the way inside her home. From there, she closes her front door and presses me up against it. Then she kisses me with even more passion than she had inside of the car.

As much as I want to grab her and turn her around, and be the one pressing her up against something, I let her stay in control. It's not something I'm used to doing, but I sort of like it.

Leah moves to kiss my neck and remove my jacket. I help her take it off and let it sink to the ground. Then she throws off her own denim jacket. When she looks at me, there's nothing but excitement in her eyes. Not even the slightest bit of fear.

I reach for the hem of my t-shirt, giving her a questioning look. She nods her head at me, so I pull it off over my head.

She stands there for a moment to hopefully admire

my naked torso. I may not have a six-pack like my brother, but I do take good care of my body.

She moves back in and kisses me more. She starts at my lips, then moves across my jaw bone and goes to my ear, her breath sending goosebumps down my entire body.

"Brennan, I want you," she tells me. "Tonight."

29

GISELLE

When Steve calls me, his voice is frantic. I haven't heard from him since we broke up. Not once.

"Steve?" I ask outside of a modeling company's office. I'm doing some go-sees today. "What are you saying? I can barely understand you." Hearing how frantic he sounds is only making my heart beat faster, too.

"I was at a party last night!" he yells. "Somebody stole my phone."

"Are you drunk?" I ask. "Because you're talking to me on your phone right now."

"I went out first thing and got a new one this morning. I didn't realize until I woke up that it was missing."

I'm confused. "Okay… what does that have to do with me? Do I know who took it or something?"

"Giselle. The photos. They're still on my camera roll. The pictures of you and Eliza. They might be exposed at any moment."

My stomach drops so quickly and suddenly that I get lightheaded and lean against a dirty brick wall. "What?!"

"I am so sorry! I swear, I never meant for this to happen. I never planned on showing those photos to anyone. I don't know why I didn't just delete them! I'm so fucking stupid."

"You still had the photos?" I asked. He told me he deleted them.

"I know! I know! I was going to do it, I swear. This is all my fault. I am so sorry!"

"I have to go." I hang up quickly, feeling so frozen in fear that I don't know if I will ever be able to move again. If those photos are released, not only will I be exposed, but Eliza will, too. Her husband will find out. My family will find out.

"Are you okay, Giselle?" Lonnie asks me.

I slowly shake my head.

I basically have no other choice. I do *not* want

anyone finding out about the real me, especially not without me telling those closest to me first myself.

Quickly, I text Eliza, even though we haven't spoken in some time.

Me: *Steve didn't delete the photos. Somebody stole his phone and has them. Just thought you should know.*

And as if that text wasn't already terrifying enough to send, the next thing I have to do is going to be a million times more terrifying.

I walk to my car and get inside, not wanting to be in public when I do this. Lonnie goes to his SUV that's parked right next to me. He doesn't know exactly what happened, but I'm sure he could take a guess.

With shaking fingers, I call my mom.

"Giselle? Hello!" Mom says. It's the weekend, so I'm hoping she's at home with Dad and Blair.

"Mama?" I ask, my throat dry.

"Is everything okay?" she asks, sensing my voice.

"Can you put me on speaker with Dad and Blair, please? Are they there with you?"

Holy shit! Holy shit! Holy shit! I can't believe I am doing this.

"Yeah, they're right here. Hold on." It takes a couple of seconds, but it feels like a lifetime as I sit there waiting for them.

"Hi, G!" Blair greets.

"Miss you, sweetheart," Dad says.

"I need to tell you guys something."

"Are you okay?" Blair asks.

"Yeah. No. I don't know," I start. How do I even find the words? I didn't have any time to plan this out. To do it in a special way. I have never been so terrified in my entire life. I didn't want it to be like this. But I can't risk them learning the truth before I get to talk to them first.

"Tell us what's on your mind, honey," Mom says.

"Okay. I, um… You guys—I'm gay."

There is silence for a bit. I have never had any silence feel so loud. It rings in my ears and nearly makes me go insane.

Say something! I think to myself.

"You are?" Dad asks.

" Okay!" Mom says with excitement in her voice. "Wow! I never knew…"

"I always wondered why you never had boyfriends! And you seemed to really hate Steve, too, by the way," Blair says.

I laugh as tears stream down my cheeks.

"It doesn't matter to us, Giselle," Dad says. "You know we're gonna love you no matter what."

I don't know what I had been expecting. I don't know why I ever thought they would act any other way than how they are right now. They have always loved me unconditionally and supported every dream of mine. Without them, I probably would have never been able to become a model in the first place.

"I love you guys so much," I tell them through my sobs.

"Don't cry, Giselle! You had no reason to be afraid to tell us. We would never disapprove of anything you wanted to be. You know that," Mom says.

I've just heard about it go so horribly with so many other people coming out of the closet. So many people are still afraid to come out because they know they won't be accepted. So many LGBTQ beings are afraid to be their true selves because they don't live with the supportive type of family that I do. I feel horrible for those other humans. But I am so damn lucky for the family that I have.

30

———

KENNETH

$\mathcal{D}$ad is having a blowout bash for his fifty-first birthday. It's a huge deal because he wasn't supposed to make it past the age of forty-eight.

But it's an even bigger deal to me because I was invited. And so is my sister. Not by Eliza, either. Dad sent us a group chat text asking us to be there.

So, now here my sister and I are, out on a flight heading to Quincy yet again.

"I can't believe he finally wants to see us," my sister

says. I wish her sons were with us, but it's an adult-only party, and her husband had to stay behind with them.

"I bet getting to go back to his support groups and being back in Quincy is making him open up a little," I tell her.

We're flying first class, courtesy of me, and Isabell is loving every second of it. She keeps making comments about how much more comfortable the chairs are, and how she loves how much more legroom she has. I laugh at how easy she is to please. Then I make a mental note to only buy her first-class tickets to places for her birthdays and future Christmas presents.

My sister nods her head and goes back to reading her magazine. I hit her in a brotherly way when I saw that she had bought a People magazine instead of a Sunwest Weekly one. She laughs and tells me she's bought every copy I've ever had an article in, and that this one just had an article that she had been eager to read about.

"Did you hear about that supermodel?" she asks me. "Giselle Cosgrove?"

My stomach dips. "What about her?" Of course, I already know. I've been meaning to reach out to Giselle about the news. It would be good for my magazine.

"That she came out as gay! I would have never guessed," Isabell says. "I always saw photos of her with guys at parties and whatnot. Good for her, though."

I shift uncomfortably in my seat. "Oh… yeah. Good for her."

Please don't ask me, I think to myself.

My sister gets a puzzled look on her face. "Wait a second. Isn't she friends with Eliza?"

Damn it. "I don't know," I lie.

"I think she is!" she says. "I wonder if Eliza knew about it. Not that it matters. I'm just curious. She's a good friend if she did know and kept her secret all this time."

"You know what, sis?" I ask, completely about to change the subject. It came on so suddenly, what I want to talk about. The idea had sprung out of nowhere. "I have an idea."

31

GISELLE

’m surprised that Eliza even wanted to invite me to Shawn's fifty-first birthday. I figured she would want to keep her distance from me after I decided to publicly come out about being gay. The photos of us never surfaced, and even though Steve and I have no idea who stole his phone, I am grateful to whoever has it.

I am in a private jet with my date, Katie Stewart. She has cute, pixie-cut brown hair and doe-like eyes.

She's an actress who came out as gay about five years ago. As soon as she found out that I was gay, too, she messaged me on Instagram.

"What do you think it will be like?" Katie asks me as we sit next to each other and sip on some champagne.

"I don't know. It's really hard to picture because Quincy is such a small town. But I do think that there are going to be a lot of celebrities there. Should be an interesting evening."

My stomach dips for the hundredth time as I think about seeing Eliza again. Of course, it will be just as friends. But just because I am moving on, and she is staying with her husband, doesn't mean that I don't have lingering feelings. And it's sort of weird to go from seeing someone almost every day to going multiple weeks without any contact at all. Eliza hasn't been in the news much, and I'm almost totally forgetting what she even looks like.

"Tomorrow, I'm going to post on my Instagram story that I was here in Quincy, just to see which fans freak out about the fact that I was so close, and they didn't even know it!" Katie says beside me, chuckling.

I shake my head and drain the rest of my champagne, then our pilot tells us that we are about to land.

Katie takes my hand and gives it a squeeze. "It's going to be kick-ass," she tells me.

I kiss her on the cheek. "You're right. It will."

BRENNAN

I'm not much of a tuxedo guy, so I had to rent the one that I am adjusting in my bedroom mirror at my parents' right now. It's not every day I'm invited to a celebrity black-tie birthday event.

I stop adjusting my collar when I see my phone ringing on my bed. I pick it up and answer Leah's call.

"Are you excited for tonight?" she asks me.

At just the sound of her voice, I immediately wish I was alone with her again. Going all the way with Leah that night had been one of the most memorable experiences of my life. And the way we both just lied there on her bed afterward, just holding each other and talking about nothing, had been almost as wonderful as actually *doing* the deed. For some reason, everything about being with Leah is perfect.

"Define *excited*," I say to her.

She laughs, making me smile. "It will be fun, I promise!" she says. "But I think I have to meet you there; is that okay? My Friday group sessions usually run a little late, but I will come as quickly as possible."

"You want me to go *alone*?!" I ask, feeling sweaty already in this outfit.

"You'll be fine. Just drink, have snacks, blend in. Kenneth will be there, I think. Maybe hang out with him or Blair? Or hide on the back patio until I get there."

"You're lucky I like you."

"Trust me, I know."

I smile again, and we hang up. I go back to adjusting my outfit in the mirror. This is bound to be an interesting night.

33

DAMASCUS

I won't be caught dead in a penguin suit. I told Shawn this when he invited me to his birthday party in the first place. He laughed and told me it was fine, and that I could come naked for all he cared. I didn't want to look totally foolish, especially since there would be celebrities there like Blair's sister, Giselle Cosgrove, so I did something I hate doing and went *shopping*. I picked out a pin-striped, vintage-looking suit. While it is much more my style, it's still the most dressed-up I think I've ever been in my entire life.

"Oh, my goodness," Blair says when she sees me. The only reason I haven't said anything about her outfit is because I'm speechless. She's wearing a gold gown that drips along the floor. It hangs off her body in a sophisticated and sexy way, making her look even hotter than a supermodel. She's taller because she's wearing heels, too. Her hair is in some sort of braided twisted updo that looks like it took hours to do. I can't do anything but stand there and stare at her.

"You look so good," Blair says, carefully walking toward me inside my apartment and kissing me on the cheek. Then she giggles. "Oops, I'm going to have to be careful. I got lipstick on you."

Andy and Sara are out on a date tonight, so we have the apartment to ourselves. I beam at my girlfriend as she wipes her dark purple lipstick off of my cheek. I almost wish she wouldn't.

"Cat got your tongue?" she asks me with a wink as she steps back.

"You have to be the prettiest woman in the whole entire universe," I finally tell her.

She blushes instantly, and does a little twirl to show me the backless part of the dress. "Thank you," she tells me.

"You're welcome."

"Let's hurry up and go to this thing before I can no longer walk in these shoes."

"Oh, wait one second." I turn and head down the hall to my room. Then I go to the first drawer on my dresser and open it, pulling something out that I want to give to her. I walk out of my bedroom slowly, feeling slightly in a daze. I keep the object hidden behind my back as I exit the hallway and step toward her.

"I want to give you something," I tell her. I never thought in a million years that I would do something like this, but I am a hundred percent certain that I want to do it now.

She eyes me curiously. "Okay."

"I'm not saying you have to wear it tonight or anything, but your gold dress made me think of it," I tell her. "It's not anything expensive or fancy, but it's important to me."

She tilts her head at me and waits. Exhaling slowly, I reveal the thin gold chain necklace that I had been holding in my fist behind my back. I show it to her, opening it up in my palm.

She gasps and steps forward to take a closer look.

"I didn't keep very much of my brother's belongings," I explain to her. "But my parents gave this to him when he was younger, and he wore it every single day."

She puts a hand over her mouth in shock. It makes me smile to see how hesitant she is. It only makes me want her to have it more.

"I was wondering if you could keep it safe for me?"

She shakes her head. "Damascus... I couldn't!"

I shrug. "I think you could."

"This is your *brother's* necklace?" she asks, finally removing her hand from her mouth.

I nod. "I think he would really like knowing that you're wearing it. I just want him to know how happy I am, and in a way, I feel like giving this to you would help me do that."

She turns around and gets any loose hair off of her neck. She wants me to put it on her.

"You really want to wear it now? You don't have to."

"Yes, I do."

I chuckle lightly and put it on her. When she turns around, I am overwhelm with my feelings for her.

"Blair Cosgrove, I love you. So much."

Her eyes glistening, she rushes up and kisses me on the lips. "I love you, too," she breathes when she pulls away. Then she giggles again and re-wipes off the lipstick from my lips.

34

GISELLE

When I'm greeted by Shawn at the party, I expected him to be happy to see me. I expected him to tell me how pretty I look and how happy he is that I am here, and that he is happy for me for coming out of the closet and bringing a date.

Instead… it is *so* not the case.

"Why are you here with a date?" he asks with his eye-controlled computer on his chair.

He looks amazing with a fresh haircut and a classic

black and white suit. It breaks my heart to see him like this in his chair, his ALS so far progressed, but I try to remain positive about the fact that he's made it this far. He was only supposed to live to forty-eight, after all. And he blew those odds out of the water.

His question totally catches me off guard. "What are you talking about?" I ask. My date, the famous Katie Stewart, is off getting us drinks and mingling with some people that she recognized.

"It was dumb of you," Shawn says.

I pout at him. "I know it's your birthday and all, but you don't have to be so rude. What's wrong with Katie?"

"Nothing is wrong with Katie. She seems like a lovely woman. But I did not intend for you to bring a plus one."

I tilt my head at him and cross my arms. I have absolutely no idea what he's getting at.

"Eliza talked to me," he continues. "She told me how she feels about you."

"Shawn, I—"

"I'm not finished," he interrupts. "I want her to be happy. I want you to be happy. We both agreed that it is time for her to move on and be happy with you. She was scared at first, and I'm sure this is a shock to you as well, but all I want is for her to have somebody by her side when I go. I want the transition to be as easy as possible."

I am a stuttering, stammering, dry-mouthed mess. "I... You—wait a second. You know about me and Eliza? And you want... You *want* us to be together?"

His computer must be malfunctioning because there is just no way.

"I know you love her. And she loves you a great deal," he says.

"Shawn… I don't know what to say."

"Hey. At least she's not leaving me for another man."

We laugh together, and I give him a playful smirk. I've been looking around me for Eliza all night but have yet to see her. There are easily over a hundred people in this A-frame cabin, but usually, I'm able to find her in a crowd in an instant.

"Looks like you have a choice to make tonight," Shawn says.

I nod my head slowly at him.

But he has no idea.

35

KENNETH

*E*liza hugs us excitedly when we enter Dad's new digs.

"This is much more his style," Isabell says as the two of them break apart. Eliza looks lovely in a white jumpsuit, and my sister is more dressed up than I've ever seen her, in a ruffled red gown. I am in a smart navy-blue suit, my hair gelled back. Isabell told me I look like Jack Dawson on *Titanic*.

"Don't you love it?" Eliza asks. "I feel more at

home here than I ever did at the beach house." Then she looks back and forth at the two of us with a strange expression on her face. My stomach dips.

"So, where is he?" my sister asks. We're still by the front door, and before us, is an incredibly massive group of people. The A-frame cabin looks more like the lobby of a ski resort.

Eliza presses her hands together in front of her chest and grimaces. "I might have done it again."

"Done what?" my sister snaps.

"I texted you from your dad's phone. I wasn't sure you would come, otherwise. Especially you, Isabell."

Isabell looks completely betrayed. "He didn't invite us?"

"I know it was rough when it happened on Christmas last year, but this time will be different," our stepmom tries.

"Eliza," I scoff.

"Unbelievable." Isabell starts backing away. "We don't deserve this, Eliza. We never did anything wrong. It's not our fault."

"Oh, but I agree with you!"

She goes to continue, but Isabell holds up a hand to stop her. "I need to get drunk. Now." She leaves Eliza and me, and heads through the crowd.

Eliza sighs heavily. It takes her a while to sneak a peek at me. "I suppose you're mad at me, too?"

"I'm disappointed. But I'm not mad," I say. "Part of me sort of expected this. It seemed too good to be true. But regardless, I'd come anyway."

Eliza's eyebrows clash together. "What do you mean?"

"If you had told me that he wasn't going to know about it, I would've still come. I don't care if Dad doesn't *want* me around. He *needs* me around." I look at the crowd again. "Will you go fetch him?" I ask. "And I'll go find Izzy. We all need to have a talk."

"Meet us in the back bedroom. It's just down there, to the left." She points at a long hallway. I nod, and we break apart.

It takes nearly an arm and a leg for me to get Isabell to come have this talk with me, but after taking two shots with her and letting her carry a cocktail in her hand as we head down the hall, she seems more willing.

I knock softly on the door, and Eliza opens it.

Isabell inhales shortly at the sight of Dad. She hasn't seen him in a couple of years. Even I—who has seen him more recently—am overwhelmed by what he looks like. His long hair is gone. His body is frail as it sits in his wheelchair. He looks thin and tired. I have never been more painfully aware until this moment of how little time I have left with him.

"Hello, children," Dad says through his computer. Eliza closes the door behind us as I grab Isabell's hand and pull her further into the room toward him. Already, Isabell is crying silently beside me.

"Hi, Dad," she sniffs.

I nod my head at him.

"Eliza says you want to talk," he says.

"Yeah, Dad. Let me just dive right in," I start. "You have no right to keep us away from you."

I stop and wait to see if he's going to tell me that I need to leave again. To see if he's going to cut me off and disappoint us both. Instead, he does nothing.

Feeling emotional, I continue. "We are your kids, and we love you. We would've had to take care of you someday, anyway. Sure, it happened sooner than any of us would have liked. But that's no reason to push us out of your life."

Tears stream down my father's face for the first time that I ever remember seeing. Even Eliza gasps. She's quick to grab a tissue off of the nightstand and wipe his tears for him since he can no longer do it himself.

He looks at his computer to reply back to me. "I just didn't want you to remember me like this," his computer voice says.

Isabell bursts into sobs and races to his side to hold his hand in hers, sinking to her knees. I join in and sink down beside her, putting my arm around her. Together, the three of us sit there and cry. Finally, after all of these years, we have been reunited.

36

DAMASCUS

"Oh, great," I say when Blair and I walk into Shawn's birthday party together. I have my arm around Blair and feel somewhat like a movie star in my outfit. The only thing bumming me out is the fact that the governor and Jennifer are here. I spot them right away over by the massive fireplace the second we walk in.

Blair gives me a reassuring squeeze. "Don't worry, I can handle it."

For some reason, it feels as if giving Blair the necklace has made our bond even stronger. She knows she can trust me, and she knows I don't want to be with Jennifer.

If I had seen Jennifer before Blair tonight, I would've been blown away by how beautiful she looks. Her black dress is tight on her body, and her pin-straight black hair hangs long, low on her waist, shiny under the lights on the ceiling. Her legs look a million miles long, and her smile is as beautiful as ever.

But seeing her now, she pales in comparison to how Blair looks. Every single woman in this room—celebrity or not—pales in comparison to my girlfriend.

"Let's go get a drink before she spots us," I say to Blair. But it's as if talking about her somehow triggered her super hearing powers, and Jennifer's head quickly turns from the actor she's talking to and lands on us.

"Oh, boy," Blair says as Jennifer excuses herself from the actor and her father, and begins making her way over to us. She has an angry, vengeful expression on her face.

"What the hell are you doing here with her?" Jennifer asks me. She puts a hand on her hip and tosses her hair over her shoulder, trying to appear sexy and intimidating in front of Blair. Blair only stands up taller and holds her head up high.

I feel good that I have nothing to hide from Blair anymore. "She's my girlfriend?" I say to Jennifer.

She turns to Blair. "I feel bad for you," she says. "You're always going to come in second. First, you were second to me. Now, you're second to Leah."

Blair gives her a kind smile. "Hi, Jennifer. Lovely to see you."

Jennifer barks out a sarcastic laugh. "You're a fool," she says. "Damascus is a manipulative and lying coward. He's only going to hurt you, too."

"Yeah, hi," I say. "Standing right here? And hearing everything you're saying?"

Blair moves even closer to me. "Jennifer, word of advice?" she starts. "Stop wasting your life trying to drag people down with you."

"Excuse me?" Jennifer hisses.

"You may think you have Damascus figured out," Blair says. "But you know nothing about him. He's a good person, and I'm thankful that he was able to escape from being with *you*."

I shrug and offer Jennifer a smile as she stares at me incredulously. Then Blair turns my head with her hands and kisses me deeply, right in front of her. When she pulls away, she doesn't look over to see Jennifer's reaction. "Come on, babe. Let's go get drinks."

"Bye, Jennifer," I say as Blair takes my hand and pulls me away. "I'd say nice talking to you, but it wasn't."

37

BRENNAN

This fancy party is quite well underway, and I haven't seen or heard from Leah once. Every time I try to call her, she doesn't answer. I've searched the entire party to see if she's here somewhere, and I've asked around, too. But no one has seen her arrive.

I walk out on the back deck, like she suggested, taking in the view of Quincy down below the hill. I pull out my phone and try a different person this time.

"Brennan?" Dad asks when he answers my call.

We're still not exactly on the best terms, but both he and my mother have apologized for standing up for Derek after what he did to me. I've just been a little unable to fully accept their apology yet. They chose him over me, and that sucks.

"Where's Derek at tonight?" I ask, my heart beating quicker than normal.

"Why?" Dad asks.

"Just… tell me. Where is he?"

"I don't keep tabs on his every move, Brennan. He's probably out drinking. He texted your mother a little bit ago, and she couldn't make out what he was trying to say, so we can only assume he's drunk."

I feel like the IPA I just downed is going to come right back up.

I clear my throat. "Dad, do you remember what Derek said the last time we both saw him drunk and had to go pick him up from jail?"

"What?"

"Of course, you don't," I say, shaking my head and checking my pockets for my car keys. "Leah was supposed to be here forever ago. The last time Derek was drunk, that I know of anyway, he said he wanted to kill her."

38

KENNETH

*E*ven though I had been hopeful about seeing Selena at this party, I doubted it would actually happen. She doesn't know Shawn, and she barely got to know Eliza.

But then, there she appears, in front of a great stone two-story fireplace, the fire lit and crackling behind her —a stunning vision of pale pink.

She approaches me slowly as I stand there frozen with my beer in hand.

"I was wondering if I was going to see you tonight," she tells me.

"Selena," I say. Then I reach out and hug her close to me. I don't know if she had been wanting to hug me, but I can't help myself. I am just so happy to see her. I have so much I want to say to her.

When we pull away, she looks slightly flustered.

"Did your dad invite you to this one, or did you come unannounced again?" she asks.

"Uh… he's happy I'm here. And I'm happy *you're* here."

She squints at me. "Are you?"

I squint back. "Am I happy to see you?" I ask. "Of course, I am."

I can see her gnawing on the inside of her cheeks as she looks away for a moment. "I mean… don't blame me for not quite believing that, Kenneth."

I step closer to her. "What are you talking about?"

"I'm just disappointed."

"You are?"

But of course, she is. I had talked this over with Isabell the entire plane ride, and while we were driving to our hotel after we landed. My sister told me that I was an idiot, and that there was no way Selena would have shown up in LA and at my doorstep if she didn't have feelings for me. She told me I should have asked Selena to stay. And she told me that Selena would've said yes.

"Kenny, you can be so clueless," Selena says to me.

"Selena…" I trail off.

"I thought you would come back for me," she admits. "Or that you would've stopped me at the airport. Or that when I showed up at your doorstep, you would have made a move. Something. I literally threw myself at you, only to get rejected."

I feel horrible, so I smile at her to try and turn the situation around. I don't want her to be upset with me. She has no idea how I feel about her. "I'm here now, aren't I?"

She glares at me. "Yeah, for your *dad*."

I shake my head and step closer to her again. She doesn't move away from me, so I take it as a good sign. "Come on, Lena," I say. "This is *my* dad we're talking about. Do you really think he invited me? I knew he didn't want me here. I knew from the very beginning. But I came anyway. And not only did I come back to Quincy, but I bought a house down here, too. Why do you think I would do that if my dad doesn't want to see me?"

Selena tilts her head back in surprise. I step closer to her again.

"What are you saying?" she whispers. I wrap my arms around her waist, and she places her hands on my chest and peers up into my eyes.

"I'm saying that I am here for *you*, Selena."

I man up and kiss her. The moment our lips collide, I feel stupid for taking so long to do it. Kissing Selena feels right. It feels good. It feels like... destiny.

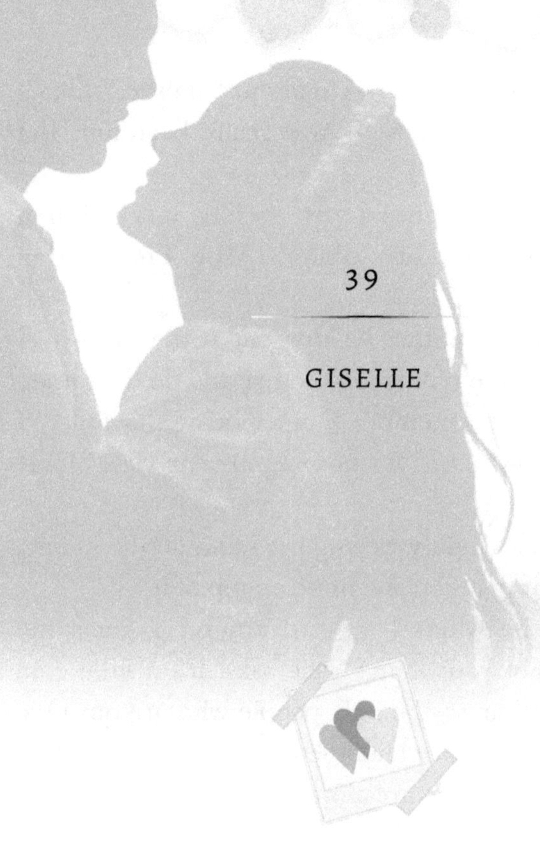

$\mathcal{E}$liza's eyes are slightly bloodshot when I finally find her out on the back porch. She's leaning against the railing by herself, looking out at the lights of our small town below.

"Hey, you," I say gently as I approach her. When she turns to look at me, she smiles weakly. "You okay?" I ask. I'm worried she's been crying over me. I don't ever want to make her upset. That will never be my intention.

"Oh, yes," she says. "I actually just finished talking with Shawn and his kids. It was really beautiful. But really sad, too."

I put a hand to my heart, feeling touched that Shawn finally spoke to his children. "Wow. I'm proud of him," I say.

She nods and resumes looking out at the town, so I lean forward on the railing next to her and do the same.

"I really don't remember Quincy being this little," I say as I look down at it. It's nothing like the view of LA from high up.

Eliza chuckles lightly. Seeing her hand on the railing, I go out on a limb and place mine on top of it.

Stunned, she whirls her head around to meet my gaze. "What are you doing?" she asks. It's a little cold and windy outside, so the only people who are out here are off in the distance, huddled by a heat lamp and smoking. Over here, we are alone.

"Eliza… I talked to Shawn."

She sighs. "Of course, you did. But then you came here with somebody else."

"I thought I was supposed to get over you," I tell her. "You sold your house in LA and just… left me there. You didn't even speak to me. I didn't think you wanted to have anything to do with me anymore."

"In a way, as horrible as it is, I'm glad that Shawn's phone was stolen."

"What do you mean?"

"If he hadn't, I might not have ever had that talk with Shawn. I might not have ever told him how I felt about you, and I might have cut off all communication with you. I felt horrible for hurting him. Even if he didn't know it, I thought I was hurting him anyway. I hadn't expected him to be so… understanding."

She gives my hand a squeeze, and I squeeze it back. "I guess that makes sense."

"I just had this idea in my head," she goes on. "It was silly of me. But I thought you would come here tonight, and I would take you out here and confess how in love with you I am, and that we would share this romantic moment, and I would finally get to be with you. It was stupid of me."

I freeze. "Wait, *what*?"

She waves her other hand at me dismissively. "Well, it doesn't matter now, does it? Since you have that young actress date of yours…"

"Oh my gosh, Liza. You can be so incredibly ridiculous sometimes." I laugh and whirl her around to face me. Then I run my fingers through her silky hair and pull her into me so I can kiss her.

She hesitates at first, but within seconds, she melts into me and wraps her arms around my waist. I am so engrossed in her touch, so overwhelmed at the fact that she just admitted she's in love with me, that I don't even hear someone approaching us.

"Oh my gosh."

Eliza and I break apart, and their Katie is.

Eliza's hand flies to her mouth in guilty shock. Katie stares at her with her eyes wide.

"Eliza Leon," Katie continues. Then she bursts into a grin. "I am so happy to finally meet you!" She reaches her hand out to shake it, and Eliza takes it with a confused expression on her face.

"Um, hello," Eliza says slowly, looking at me.

Katie waves off the fact that we just kissed. "Oh, she must not have told you yet," she says to Eliza. "Giselle just brought me here to make you jealous. And she promised that, in return, I would get to meet you and chat with you."

Eliza's mouth drops open in surprise, and she turns to me. "Is this true?"

I giggle and shrug. "Guilty as charged!"

40

BRENNAN

I don't even feel a little bit bad when I see Selena and Kenneth making out in a corner and go interrupt them. I'm too panicked to care about anything.

I break them apart with my hands, so terrified that I can barely see straight. "Kenneth. It's Leah," I manage.

Their happy faces fall immediately when they see mine. "What's wrong?" Selena and Kenny ask together.

I can barely get another word out. I stand there feeling dizzy.

Kenneth clasps a hand on my shoulder. "Brennan, what happened?" he tries again.

"She's not here," I say. "She's not here, and Derek is drunk."

Thankfully, this is all I needed to say. I watch as both of their eyes grow with the realization of what I'm trying to tell them.

"Where is she?" Kenneth asks in a serious voice.

"I think she's at her apartment. Or I don't know, at the town center even?" I hope she's there, anyway. I hope she's okay.

"Is she not answering her phone?" Selena asks. I shake my head and swallow back the vomit that keeps trying to come up. I don't know how to express to them that I don't want to stand here and play Twenty Questions. I just want to get to Leah.

Kenneth digs around his suit and pulls out his car keys. "Alright, let's go."

Together, the three of us race toward the front door of Shawn and Eliza's home.

41

DAMASCUS

Blair and I are talking to Shawn when we notice Brennan approaching Kenneth and Selena over in the corner. We had been spying on them because Shawn was surprised to see Kenneth—his son —making out with the woman. Shawn said he had no idea that they were together because Eliza had informed him when they ran into him on Christmas day that they were just friends.

"What's happening over there?" Blair asks. "Brennan looks like he's going to throw up."

Shawn speaks from his computer. "Leah isn't here," he tells us.

I look at Blair. Realization seems to hit us at the same time.

"Does that mean…?"

"It's probably not good to jump to any conclusions, but something is wrong." Shawn pauses for a moment, then he has his computer talk again. "I am scared."

Now I'm scared for Leah, too. It's not like Leah to not show up for Shawn. And after I kissed her, and she punched me in the face that one day at the hospital, she explained to me how Derek had hurt her, and how trau-matized she had been by him in the past. She even mentioned to me that she didn't feel safe knowing he was out and about walking freely.

I look at Shawn. "What can we do?" I ask.

He looks at his computer screen to talk. "Keep Leah safe."

42

BRENNAN

'm grateful that Kenneth has offered to drive because, not only have I had more than my limit of drinks, but I am also too afraid to. I'm so paralyzed by my fear of what Derek could have possibly done to Leah, that when Selena and Kenneth talk to each other in the front seat, I don't even hear what they're saying.

I punched Leah's address into Kenneth's phone so

that he could easily get to her house without me trying to attempt to bark out the directions. I want to check there first instead of where she holds her meetings because I'm not even sure if Derek knows that she runs support groups.

It feels like we hit every single red light, but every time we come across one, Kenneth makes sure that nobody is coming, and then he runs it. I have the window rolled down—even though it's cold outside—so that I can hurl out the window if I need to. I stick my head out as we pull into Leah's neighborhood and get closer to her street. I'm terrified that I'm going to see Derek's car out in front of her place once we turn the corner.

When Kenneth finally turns, it's worse than I imagined.

There are fire trucks, ambulances, cop cars, and police tape everywhere. I don't see what happened right away because of the blinding red and blue lights, but when we get closer, I forget to breathe.

There is my brother's SUV, halfway sticking out of Leah's living room. He had driven his car straight through her home.

"Holy shit," Kenneth says.

"That's Derek's car!" Selena cries out in case we didn't already know.

Kenneth parks the car, and the two of them climb out. I am too stunned to move.

They're dead. Leah and Derek are dead. How could they not be? Her small two-bedroom home is nearly fully engulfing his car. The only parts of it that look unhit are where her bedroom and her garage are.

"Brennan, come on!" Selena snaps at me, opening my car door and grabbing my arm. Once I'm out and on my feet, I race past both of them. I need to find an officer. I need to know where Leah is. Where my brother is.

"Brennan!" Kenneth calls after me.

"Leah!" somebody yells. Their voice sounds like a wounded animal, and quickly, I realize it's coming from my own mouth.

I run toward the yellow police tape and try to duck under it, but a police officer is quick to grab my arms and pull me back.

"What do you think you're doing?!" he yells.

"Leah!" I shout again.

"Brennan! Over here!" Kenneth calls. I break out of the cop's grip and run in the other direction toward Kenneth's voice. There, sitting in the back of an ambulance, is Leah. Tears are streaming down her face, and she has a blanket draped over her.

"Thank, God," I breathe out, running over to her. I can't get there fast enough.

Leah's eyes widen when she sees me, and she only cries harder. I wrap my arms around her and hold her close. She hugs me back.

"Are you okay?" I ask. "Did he hurt you?"

She shakes her head. "I'm fine, I'm fine."

"Where is Derek?" Selena asks, tears in her eyes, too.

"He's already taken away in a police car," Leah explains.

"What the hell happened?" Kenneth asks.

"I don't know," Leah says. "I don't know if it was intentional, or if Derek lost control of his car. I was just getting ready in my room, and I heard a super loud crashing noise. I walk out into my hallway, and there Derek is, barely conscious in his car."

I hug her again. I want to hug her a thousand more times. I'm so thankful she was in her bedroom when Derek did this, and I don't even want to think about what he would have done to her if he hadn't crashed his car. I don't know what his intention was, but I know it wasn't anything good.

"Your brother is just sad and depressed," Leah tells me. "He's been caught, and nobody believes he's not abusive. He's already going to get everything taken away from him. So, I'm not going to press charges."

"Are you *insane*?" I bellow.

She sniffs and wipes her eyes. "I'm getting a restraining order, but I'm not pressing charges. I'm not doing that to you and your family."

I shake my head, bewildered. "Don't do it for me. Don't do anything for me or my family. *Screw* us. He needs to go to prison! He could've killed you, Leah!"

"It doesn't matter, Brennan. You heard what my dad said. He has good lawyers. He will get out of whatever situation he gets put in. He will worm his way out of this one, too. And I've already spent so much of my life fighting against him. I don't want to do it anymore."

Then she wraps her arms around me and cries into my chest. "Please don't let me go, Brennan."

I hold her tightly to me and look at Kenneth and Selena. They look just as shocked as I feel.

"It's okay, Leah," I say into her hair. "He is never going to touch you again."

43

GISELLE

I am happier than I have ever been in all of my existence. I have truly reached the pinnacle of a perfect life. I have my dream job. I have my dream partner—Eliza, of course. And I am out of the closet and proud of it. Sure, I've lost lots of fans, but in place of them, I've gained thousands of new ones. I am being supported in ways I never even thought was possible. And I am more inspirational than ever, apparently.

"Are you ready to do this thing?" Eliza asks me from inside her A-frame house in Quincy.

"This *thing*?" I ask, timidly stepping closer to her. She looks beautiful in her black dress, black tights, and stylish black hat. "Eliza, are you sure you're alright?"

She sniffs and smiles at me. "Yes," she lies. She's been crying on and off all day. I kiss her swiftly on the lips.

"You can do this," I tell her reassuringly.

She nods and kisses me again. Eliza came out to the public two months ago, and she's already been photographed with me in several places. Right now, we are currently trending on social media. We are one of Hollywood's new "it" couples, apparently. Lots of people think our love story is some huge scandal, which in some ways, it is. Eliza has been given lots of hate, and so have I, but the only thing that matters is that the people who are close to us support us. And if Shawn were still alive, he'd be supporting us, too.

I pull my phone out and check my incoming message. "The car is here, Liza."

Eliza spritzes on some perfume, wipes her eyes in the mirror—careful not to mess up her makeup—then takes my hand. Together, we walk out of the house, get into the town car, and head to Shawn Geiger's funeral.

44

KENNETH

Six months later…

I'm feeling pretty sad today, but it could be worse. At least I knew it was coming, and I got the chance to say goodbye to my father. Thankfully, I have Selena by my side because I don't know how I would do this without her.

"You know, I'm glad we decided to keep this place,"

Selena says as she rubs my back while I am putting on my dress shoes.

We are currently in our townhome in Quincy. We don't get to visit that often, but I agree that it's nice to have a place to escape to. Selena is still trying to adjust to life in LA, anyway. And it's even more difficult to do when she's three months pregnant.

Selena and I moved fast, but it wasn't all on purpose. Two months into dating, Selena and I decided to go on a trip to Las Vegas. There, we had one drink too many and found ourselves getting married by someone dressed in an Elvis costume. We barely remembered it the next day, but we had photos to prove it. And giggling over brunch, we decided to stay married. We undoubtedly one hundred percent knew we were in love with each other, and that we wanted to be together forever.

Then a month later, she told me that she had forgotten to take her birth control for three days in a row, but neither of us took precautions. I've always wanted to be a dad, and Selena would make the perfect mother.

"Now, we have two bedrooms we have to decorate," I remind her with a smile.

It's strange; I first found out that Selena was pregnant just a couple months ago, then very shortly after, I found out that my father was finally going to pass. I am in this weird in-between state of mourning his loss and being excited for the birth of my child. And it's greatly depressing to me that my child won't ever get to know his grandfather.

"But he will know of him through your stories and memories," Selena had told me.

Again, I know I can't do any of this without her beside me. She is my perfect dream girl, and I never plan on letting her go.

45

———

BRENNAN

Six months later…

I hold Leah's hand the second we step out of the car and head to the funeral, and I don't let go of it once. The service hasn't started yet, so everyone is talking to one another and giving their condolences to each other.

Leah and I are both excited to see Kenneth and

Selena again—they don't come to Quincy often, but every time they do, we meet up for a double date. I can't believe they're already married and pregnant because it feels like Leah and I are still so far from that.

As in love with Leah as I am, we are still taking things very slowly. I finally moved out of my parents' house and bought a place of my own—walking distance to my shop, actually. Leah and I haven't moved in together yet, but I wonder if it could be coming up shortly because she is over at my place basically every single day. She even has a toothbrush and a drawer to herself in my bedroom.

"The service will be starting in five minutes," a man says over a microphone inside of the church we've gathered in.

"I guess we should go find our seats," Leah says to me with teary eyes. I kiss her forehead in support. She admired Shawn very much.

When I back away from her, my eyes fly to a cocky-looking guy who's wearing his sunglasses still, even though he's inside. He has his hands on his hips and is smiling around the room like this is a wedding event and not a funeral.

"Oh, no," I say, stones dropping in my stomach.

I almost wish I could shield Leah from this sight. She does *not* need this today. She's already having a difficult time enough as it is, trying to get over her trauma with Derek crashing his car into her living room.

Leah turns around and almost jumps at the sight of her ex-abuser and my brother. "What is Derek doing here?" she whispers to me.

"I don't know," I tell her truthfully. "But it can't be anything good. I'll go get rid of him; don't worry." I let go of her to walk in his direction, but then I pause. Selena has beaten me to it. She approaches him quickly, and quicker than the blink of an eye, she punches him in the face. All around, people gasp.

"You have no right coming here!" she screams at him. "Get the *fuck* out!"

I race over with Kenneth and a couple other guys, and together, we separate Selena and Derek.

"You crazy bitch!" my brother yells at her. I get one of his arms and Kenneth gets the other, and we drag him back down the aisle toward the exit.

"Dude, you just got punched by a pregnant lady," Kenneth says with an amused smile. I shake my head, knowing that finding out that his ex-wife is pregnant is only going to get him more riled up. In our arms, Derek fights to break free. With no football and hardly any fame anymore, Derek has nearly whittled down to nothing. He's the one who lives in my parents' house now. He works at the grocery store. He spends his time in and out of rehab.

"Good thing Selena got to you when she did, bro," I say as I struggle to keep hold of him. "Because you were about three steps away from breaking your restraining order with my girlfriend."

"Screw all of you!" Derek shouts. It's clear he came here just to stir up some drama. My brother has always loved getting attention, after all.

"Do you know what, Brennan?" Kenneth asks. "I think he *did* break the restraining order."

If getting my brother arrested is going to keep him away from us, I'm game. "Oh, wait," I say. "That's right. Hang onto him, will you?" I motion for some other guys to help. Then I get on my phone and call the police.

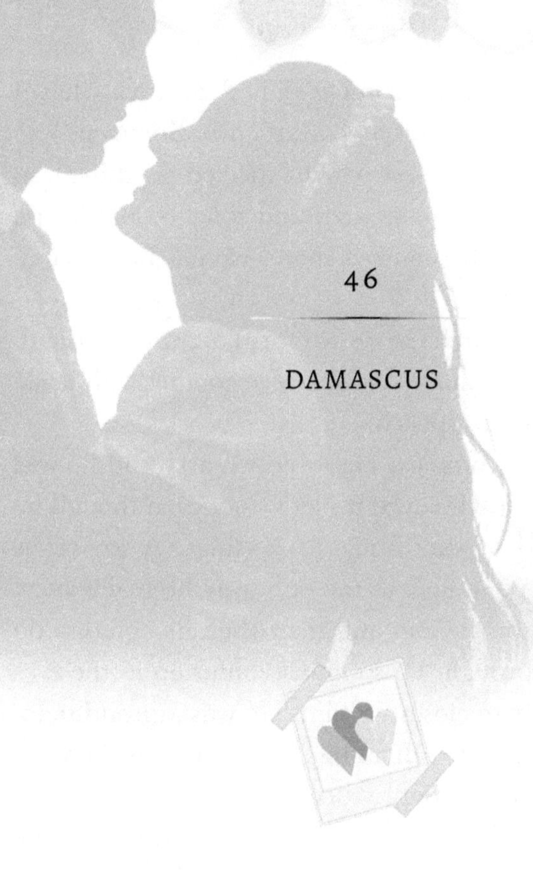

46

———

DAMASCUS

Six months later…

Up at the microphone, I clear my throat and look at everyone. It feels hot in here with all the light shining on me as I wear this stupid dress shirt and these pants. There are a lot more people here than I thought there would be, too. But Shawn asked me to speak, so I'm going to speak. I will do anything for that man.

"Thank you all for coming. I had no idea Shawn knew this many people," I start off. Some people chuckle. "But I don't know why I expected anything less. Shawn was a phenomenal man and touched the hearts of many lives. Of course, there would be a large crowd."

I pause and search the crowd for Blair, my girlfriend. As long as I can continue to make eye contact with her, I can get through this speech.

"Shawn was complex. He loved his art. And he was able to show that. He loved his kids, too, even though he wasn't as good at expressing his feelings. A lot of us could say that painting was the only way he really knew how to share how he felt, and that when he couldn't do it anymore, it brought up so much confusion in the eyes of those who were closest to him. He was a proud man, stubborn as hell, but with a huge heart. He was there for me at our support group… because I had recently lost my brother to ALS before I met him. Leah Olson, the great support group leader that she is, almost seemed like a student whenever Shawn was in class. He was so wise and had so much to say. So many tips to share and knowledge to spread. Leah and I are so grateful for everything we learned from him."

I take a short pause to reel in my tears and clear my throat before continuing. "I can't help but think about the diversity of the people inside of this church today. It seems crazy to me that all of these different lives are brought together by this one, single, wonderful—even though he was a hard-ass—human. There's me, who is an outsider in this town and only happened to be here by chance. My girlfriend, Blair, a college student who got to meet him because of me, and because of her sister, a *supermodel,* mind you. Giselle Cosgrove knew Shawn well and considered him a very close friend. Some of you may know this, but now, she's dating Shawn's widowed wife, Eliza Leon."

I pause again and wait for some of the murmurings to die down. The two of them together is definitely a controversial subject. "And to clear the air on that matter, Shawn *wanted* them to be together. He talked to them separately about it before he passed. I'm happy as hell for them, and you all should be, too." I turn my head and smile at them both.

"And Shawn brought two wonderful kids into the world, who are much older than me. Kenneth and Isabell. Kenneth is a celebrity journalist. He lives in LA, just like Giselle does. Just like Eliza does. Just like good man Shawn used to. And Shawn's son introduced his wife to him—Selena. And it was Derek Heed—as unfortunate as that quasi-famous man is—who led her here and into Kenneth's life in the first place. Then there's Steve, who is not only Kenneth's good friend, but Giselle Cosgrove's ex-boyfriend. And look at him—he's found himself a small-town woman to date! That's his date next to him—Jennifer, my ex."

The coincidence is insane to me, but apparently, Jennifer and Steve met at the New Year's Eve party in The Warehouse, and Steve found her on social media and messaged her shortly after ending things with Giselle.

"Steve is a celebrity photographer, and Jennifer is

the governor's daughter! I mean, honestly. What is the world if not just a spherical globe composed of millions of little coincidences? You could almost say, as I like to think, that everything that has happened to us was meant to bring us to this moment. It sucks to lose the people you love, but I genuinely believe we are all exactly where we are supposed to be. And all of us are here now because one single man affected so many lives. Shawn Geiger is a huge part of the reason I'm following in my brother's footsteps and becoming a firefighter. He wanted nothing but to see everyone around him succeed. Shawn Geiger lives on in all of us. And I am so eternally grateful to have known him. Thank you."

EPILOGUE

In the end, Shawn got to do what many people couldn't before he died. He got to record a speech for everyone from his computerized chair. And because of that, Shawn was able to say goodbye.

After Damascus steps off the stage, and the room explodes in applause over his speech, Eliza, Kenneth, and Isabell get on the stage and hook up the computer to play Shawn's final message, the words of what his computerized voice says displaying on the projector screen behind his closed coffin.

"I think it's pretty great that I can share one last message with everybody. If there is one thing I want you all to learn from being here today, it's not just that I was a really good painter. It's that time is precious. Nobody seems to understand that until it's too close to the end. Time is precious, and not a single second of it should be wasted. Wasted because of anger. Wasted because of bitterness. Wasted because of pride. Wasted because of sadness. Or even, damn it, wasted because of sheer laziness."

"Don't ever say, 'I will do it tomorrow,' to anything of significant importance to you. Don't wait to call your friends and family. Don't wait to sign up for that new class or get that new haircut. Don't chicken out and wait another moment to tell your crush that you like them. Don't waste any chance to tell somebody that you love them. Don't hesitate to apologize. You have to learn from my mistakes. If you don't, I will have died for nothing. I made all of these mistakes. Every single one of them. And I will never get to redo any of them. I'll never get a chance to fix things. And that is something I take full responsibility for. But I love my wife and children more than life. And I hope, despite the poor choices that I've made in the past, that they all know that. If there is one regret I never had for a single moment, it was getting to be their husband and father."

"Each moment is a treasure. Hang on to the moments, no matter how insignificant they may seem at the time. You will be a much happier person if you do. Thank you all for such a wonderful life."

When Shawn Geiger's speech ends, and the slideshow of him and his family and friends starts up on the projector screen, there is not a single dry eye in the entire church.

The End

STALK KATHRYN REIGN BELOW!

Website:

https://www.kathrynreign.com/

Facebook Page:

https://www.facebook.com/authorkathrynreign

Instagram:

https://www.instagram.com/authorkathrynreign/

Goodreads:

https://www.goodreads.com/author/show/
21854875.Kathryn_Reign

BookBub:

https://www.bookbub.com/authors/kathryn-reign

VALENTINE VOWS

BOOK THREE OF THE MISSED CONNECTIONS TRILOGY

KATHRYN REIGN